Praise for Mark Brandi

Wimmera

Winner, 2016 DEBUT DAGGER, UK Crime Writers' Association
Winner, 2018 DEBUT FICTION AWARD, Indie Book Awards
Shortlisted, 2018 BEST DEBUT CRIME, Ned Kelly Awards
Shortlisted, 2018 LITERARY FICTION BOOK OF THE
YEAR, Australian Book Industry Awards
Shortlisted, 2018 MATT RICHELL AWARD FOR NEW
WRITER OF THE YEAR, Australian Book Industry Awards

'The reader is in the hands of a master storyteller . . . This is
literary crime fiction at its best'

Books+Publishing

'Very little fiction is as emotionally true as this. *Wimmera* is a
dark and disturbing story from a substantial new talent'

The Saturday Paper

'What makes *Wimmera* so effective, and original, is the pacing
and restraint'

Sydney Morning Herald

'Subtle and devastating. The novel crackles with suspense
and dread'

Australian Book Review

'*Wimmera* makes excellent use of atmospheric rural Australia to
weave a gothic story with a strongly rooted sense of place'

Herald Sun

The Rip

'*The Rip* pulled me into its unpredictable waters, and refused to let go; authentic, heartfelt . . . and original'

SOFIE LAGUNA

'[an] accomplished second novel that certainly live[s] up to the promise of the first'

Sydney Morning Herald

'stripped-back and intimate . . . there's no doubting the skill with which Brandi ratchets up the tension'

The Weekend Australian

'A superb book – beautifully conceived, masterfully executed. A winner'

CHRIS HAMMER

'a fast-paced crime novel full of dread and suspense'

Herald Sun

'another tension builder'

Courier Mail

'What held me close in this novel was not the idea of a hidden population of drifters and addicts, but the writer's reassurance that dignity and small kindnesses have a place in that world'

JOCK SERONG

The
Others

Also by Mark Brandi

Wimmera

The Rip

The Others

MARK BRANDI

hachette
AUSTRALIA

This project has been assisted by the Australian Government through the Australia Council, its arts funding and advisory body.

 Supported by the City of Melbourne COVID-19 Arts Grants.

This project is supported by the Victorian Government through Creative Victoria and by UNESCO Melbourne City of Literature.

Published in Australia and New Zealand in 2021
by Hachette Australia
(an imprint of Hachette Australia Pty Limited)
Level 17, 207 Kent Street, Sydney NSW 2000
www.hachette.com.au

10 9 8 7 6 5 4 3 2 1

 A catalogue record for this book is available from the National Library of Australia

ISBN: 978 0 7336 4114 5 (paperback)

Cover design by Christabella Designs
Cover photographs courtesy of Shutterstock
Author photograph courtesy of Julian Dolman
Text design by Bookhouse, Sydney
Printed and bound in Australia by McPherson's Printing Group

The paper this book is printed on is certified against the Forest Stewardship Council® Standards. McPherson's Printing Group holds FSC® chain of custody certification SA-COC-005379. FSC® promotes environmentally responsible, socially beneficial and economically viable management of the world's forests.

For my father

I don't think of you much anymore.

No one really knows about you. Only Sam, and she can't tell anyone. I don't have many friends. Don't need them. You taught me that.

Even if I did have friends, I couldn't tell them.

Good thing is, people around here don't ask too many questions. And what they don't know, they make up, which is fine by me. Plus, the rent's cheap.

The reminders are less frequent nowadays, less keenly felt. More often, if I'm honest, I'm searching for the feeling. Just to feel something.

It's as though if I don't feel it anymore, it isn't real. Sometimes I tell myself that's true.

But then, other times, it comes from nowhere. Like something sticking in my guts. Even after all these years.

It took me a long time to realise what happened, even if I've never really understood. When I was a kid, I thought everything would be okay. That you might come back and make things all right again. That they might help you, and you'd get better too. I didn't realise what I was feeling was grief. Sam's helped with that. Before therapy, I didn't know I was allowed to feel that sorrow. For what I lost, and for what I never had.

Didn't know I was allowed to, because of the things you did. The things I found out.

I also felt guilt. Guilt about what happened. But that's getting better.

Or it was. Until last night. And then today.

Last night I read a news story – it was a similar case, but not the same. They're never exactly the same. And only sometimes do I get a mention. Just for a local angle, I guess.

Has similarities to . . .

Reminiscent of . . .

Like the infamous . . .

I read the article. Read it again. Searched for other reports. I only had a minute before I had to get back on my shift. I do night shifts, mostly. Better money, less talk.

It wasn't the same. None could ever be the same as us.

What you did.

What I did too.

•

I woke up and had a feeling – a feeling of you being near.

When I shut my eyes, I could almost see you.

Your gold tooth.

Can't remember exactly what you look like anymore. And you'd be different now anyway, if you're still out there.

You're a spectre, drifting into my thoughts without a proper invite, then out again. Less of a trace, less form, with each passing year.

I can't remember everything, but I remember some things pretty clear.

Your anger.

The soft eyes, too.

But the *feeling* is something different. And the feeling is something I'm less able to get hold of. Can't conjure it – just comes unexpectedly.

And it wasn't the news story that did it so much.

Was something else.

And then, I saw it.

•

There's a gum tree in my backyard. A big one. When the wind's up, it creaks and cracks like it might be about to fall. Has done for ages.

My neighbour would love to see it gone. More likely to fall on me, not him. Unfortunately.

I like to look at it. I like to watch its branches in the breeze, and I look for subtle changes. The loss of bark, the beginning of a wattlebird's nest, a new sprout – all these things, I notice. You taught me to notice. You taught me on our walks.

I was drinking a coffee in the kitchen, looking out. I've always needed those moments, the quiet. More so lately.

I watched the tree, the gentle sway of its branches, the grey sky behind. And I could sense something. Something different, but I wasn't sure what.

I looked it up and down a few times, and something wasn't quite right.

And I felt it.

I felt it before I saw.

It was a broken branch – a small one, stood up between two of the larger roots, leaning against the trunk.

The sort of thing no one else would notice.

But I noticed. I noticed, because I watch that tree. And because I'm careful, like you taught me.

I knew it was a message.

I didn't finish my coffee. I went out there, into the cool of the morning. I picked up the branch, studied it. There was nothing to be read from its leaves, its smooth skin.

I placed it on the ground.

I didn't want anyone else to notice, didn't want them to see what I saw.

But no one else would see, or understand – that's the whole point.

Only me and you. We're the only ones who'd know.

The only ones who knew.

And I know you might come for me.

Because I had to choose.

Because I'm one of the others.

•

You taught me a lot when I was young, a lot of things that made me who I am. Like keeping a diary – you said that would help. It'd help my writing, you said, and help keep my thoughts in order.

I've still got the old diaries, but I never look at them.

It wouldn't hurt to look now. I know what happened, of course. Most of it, at least. The facts, I mean, not the feelings.

The feelings I've kept out.

Had to.

But I remember some of the things you said.

I remember one thing you said, especially, more than once.

If the others come, everything will change.

You were wrong about a lot of things. Most things, really. But you were right about that.

Sam reckons I should read them. She says to understand ourselves in the present, we need the context of our past. We need to attach meaning.

'It's no good just repressing our feelings.'

That's what she tells me.

But she doesn't know everything. Everything that happened, I mean. No one knows that.

Only me and you.

If she knew everything, she might think it's better not to look back.

Because sometimes, things are better left in the past. Dangerous things. Things like you.

The branch against the gum tree is a message. I know it. I know you're watching. And now the past is here.

So I need to look back and remember what you told me, what you did.

I have to remember all about you.

I have to remember, so I'm ready.

So I'm ready if you're coming.

I'll get the rifle out too. Just in case.

In case you're coming.

Just in case you're coming for me.

part one

part one

one

This is the first page of my diary. My father gave it to me for my eleventh birthday. I know when it's my birthday, because he tells me.

I asked him what to write in here, and he said I should write about things that happen.

'In the order they happen,' he said. 'And if not much happens, you should write about your thoughts and things like that. Or describe things around the house and farm. Or things you remember.'

But he told me not to write everything. Some things, I'm not allowed to write down.

He reckons he won't read it, but that might not be true.

So I've decided I'll keep it hidden, just in case.

•

My father reckons I need to practise my writing, so I need to write in this diary as much as I can.

That's what he tells me.

diary

daily record of events or thoughts.

I probably should've put that at the start, but it's pretty much what I wrote anyway.

I asked him why I should practise, and he said it's because I mix up my tenses sometimes. The tenses are past, present, and future. He was angry in the lesson, because I got that wrong.

'What the hell's the matter with you?' he said.

I saw more of the whites of his eyes, which is what happens when he's angry. They open up really wide.

So I didn't answer.

But he thinks this diary will help things.

'It'll improve your writing,' he said. 'And help keep your thoughts in order.'

But I don't need to write everything down. He said that again, in case I didn't get the message the first time.

So here's some of my thoughts. I'll start at the beginning, because that's the right order.

We live on the farm. But my father didn't always live on the farm.

The Others

My father says he used to live in the town, but there's no way I'd be able to remember, because it was before I was born. My mother lived there too. But I only know the farm.

The town is hard to imagine, even when he describes it. He says there's people there, and the people have houses, like ours, except right up close to each other. He says it's like people have farms, except they're not much bigger than their houses, and some have fences around their houses to keep each other out. But I've never seen it.

There are roads in front of the houses, and the roads lead to the middle of the town. That's what my father told me. In the middle of the town is the town hall, where the leader lives and makes decisions. The town hall is the biggest building, bigger than all of the houses put together. This is how I imagine it, anyway.

Around the town hall are the shops.

'The shops are where you can get food and things like that,' he said. 'If you don't grow your own.'

But he never really explained how it works. I mean, why the shops give things away to people. When I asked in a lesson once, he said, 'You don't need to worry about that.'

Anyway, the town isn't near our farm.

'It's a long, long way away.'

He says it's miles away, too far for me to walk, out over the hill. He says there's hardly anyone left there anymore.

When I asked him once why he and my mother left, he said, 'We had no choice.'

That's really all he's said about it.

But there's more to the story. I know there's more, because there's somewhere else my father and mother lived too. Somewhere after the town, but before the farm. He doesn't like talking about it very much.

Anyway, it's better on the farm.

That's what he tells me.

I looked up town in the encyclopedia once, but there wasn't anything. I was hoping it would be there, so I could see a picture.

I looked it up in the dictionary and it did say a bit about it, but not in the same way my father says.

town

densely populated built-up defined area, between a city and a village in size, and having local government.

That's a picture of what I think it looks like. I used both what the dictionary says and what my father says. I use the dictionary for spelling sometimes, but for meanings too.

The other place my father said he lived was the commune, but that's what he doesn't like talking about. Even less than the town.

commune

*group of people sharing living accommodation, goods, etc.,
esp. as a political act.*

I don't really know what that means, but I can't ask about
it. I tried the other day, and he got angry.

'Just leave it!'

That's what he said when I asked, and he said it really loud.
I saw the whites of his eyes. When that happens, I know to
be quiet.

It's been happening more lately – him getting angry. He says
he's sorry after. Most times.

•

I'd like to go to the town one day. Just to see it once, to check
it against my picture. I've asked him a few times. He says I've
been there before, but was too young to remember.

I don't know if that's true.

I'm more interested in the town than the commune, but I'd
like to see that too.

I could maybe even just see the town from the top of the hill,
then check if my picture is right. I tried to sneak off once, to
look at it from the hill, but he caught me. He caught me going
up the trail, and he belted me something terrible.

He belted me with the bendy stick, which is a special branch
from a tree that's bendy and thin. He used to keep it in his

room. He belted me when we were back at the house. He pulled down my pants and my undies and belted me until I promised not to go again.

I promised.

Afterwards, he said he was sorry. He nearly always says he's sorry if he hurts me. Most times.

But he's promised not to use the bendy stick anymore.

'The sins of the father are visited upon the son,' he said.

I'm not sure what he meant by that.

He goes there sometimes, to the town I mean, but not very often. He goes to get things, like the oats, and the bullets for the rifle. But he says it's dangerous. That I can't risk going with him. Because of the others.

'Like a moth to a flame.'

Not sure what he meant by that, either.

He says he won't always be able to get things from the town, which is why the farm is important. It's important the farm is going properly again, with the sheep and the crop and the reservoir. He calls it 'the reservoir', but it's really just a big dam.

That's what I think.

I'm not sure of the exact difference between the two, but it seems like a reservoir should be bigger.

I looked it up in the dictionary, and that decided it for me. But I won't argue with him. It's best not to.

reservoir
large natural or artificial lake as a source of water supply.

I tried the encyclopedia, but forgot that R is missing. Not sure it would have had it anyway. It doesn't have everything in there, and not as many things as the dictionary. It just describes them for longer. Sometimes it has pictures.

The dictionary would be better if it had pictures.

He said I don't need to write in here every day, but I should do it as much as I can. So I am.

Most times I do what I am told. Most times.

two

There's two fingers on the mantel above the fireplace.
They're his fingers.

They're in the lounge room, where we hardly ever sit. We always sit in the kitchen. I think we used to sit in the lounge room more when my mother was here, but I can't remember exactly. She's been gone a long time.

The lounge room has a blanket my mother knitted, but I'm not allowed to touch it. He gets angry if I do. It's dark green, and it's warm and made of wool. It's on the lounge chair, which is brown and soft, but we're not allowed to sit there.

It's the fourth one and the little one. From my father's left hand. The fourth and the fifth.

They're black and dry, and the nail on the fourth one is yellow and almost see-through now. The little one hasn't got a nail, just skin and bone. I'm not sure why the little one has shrivelled up more, but it's probably not important.

Sometimes he says, 'Remember how it happened?'

I remember. It was more than a year ago. Maybe two. It happened with the big knife, the best knife we've got. He was cutting a piece of meat from a goat he'd killed out hunting. A leg, I think. Or maybe a shoulder.

When he goes out hunting, I have to stay home.

'Isn't safe,' he says. 'Not for a child.'

So I have to stay home, and I have to stay in my room. It's just in case the others come. I don't mind staying home so much, because it gives me time to do my own things.

Sometimes, I hear the gunshot from somewhere in the bush. It must be a long way away, because it takes a long time for sound to travel. I know this because he told me in one of our lessons.

'Sound travels slowly,' he said.

Lessons are usually every second day after breakfast, and it's where he tells me things, that's how I know. We have lessons in the school room, which is the room next to my bedroom. It's pretty much the same as my bedroom, except the window doesn't close properly, so it gets cold sometimes.

The school room has a blackboard, which he uses in the lessons. Sometimes, I use the blackboard to practise my drawings, but I'm not supposed to. It's only meant for words and maths.

In the school room, he teaches words and maths and about how things work. But in the afternoon sometimes, we walk outside and he tells me about nature and clouds, and tells me stories about animals and insects.

But I learn things myself too. In the encyclopedia and dictionary.

He called the goat he killed 'the beast'. He took the big knife with him, and the hessian sack.

I've only seen a goat a few times when I've been with him up the hill, and they always run off before I get a good look. But there's pictures in the encyclopedia. No pictures of a beast, though. And when I looked it up in the dictionary, it sounded different.

beast
animal, esp. a wild mammal. brutal person.

When I told him, he said, 'Some words have different meanings,' which I already knew, because he'd told me in a lesson. He told me when we talked about *practice* and *practise*, which are two different things.

Here's a picture of a goat I copied from the encyclopedia. I didn't trace it, because the background was too dark, and there was other goats next to it. Tracing is where you put paper over the top of the other picture, and the lines of the other picture show through, and you can follow them on your paper and make a copy. He showed me how in one of our lessons, but I only do it for the hard pictures.

When it happened, my father was trying to get the bone out of a piece of meat. There was a lot of blood, so the kitchen bench was slippery, and the meat slipped and the knife went into his left hand, which was holding the meat. I saw the whole thing.

The meat was on the floor, the knife slid off somewhere, and he just stood there looking at his hand. The blood squirted at first, from the stumps where his fingers had been, then ran like a stream. It mixed in with the goat blood on the floor, and was really hard to clean up after.

He looked at his hand up close, like he was unsure about it, like it wasn't really part of him or his body. Like it was just something strange that had happened, and he wanted to understand it. I couldn't stop staring even though it made me feel sick.

'Get one of my shirts,' he said. His voice sounded funny, strangled in his throat.

I got a shirt from his room and he wrapped it around his hand as tight as he could, then tied the sleeves up in a knot. I had to hold it in place when he did the knot, so he could get it tight enough to stop the blood.

The whole time he didn't say it was hurting, not once. He probably didn't need to.

I helped him pick up the meat off the floor, then his fingers too. The little one took a while to find. It had gone underneath the pot-belly stove, like it was hiding. It was bent, like it was trying to walk on its own, to get away.

At first, I thought he wanted them so they could be sewn back on. He told me once how that could be done sometimes, people could have bits sewn back together. Like the story, *Frankenstein.*

He told me about that story one day on a walk, how the woman who wrote it had a dream, then wrote about the dream. I found out more about it in the encyclopedia, about the monster who was sewn together from different bodies in a graveyard.

This is a picture of what that would look like. There's no picture in the encyclopedia, so I have to make this up.

It isn't my best picture, but I might fix it later.

•

I wasn't sure what my father was planning to do with his fingers. I didn't see them again for a long time, but I didn't forget about them. It would be strange to have part of your body separate from you. I think you'd want to keep them close.

It was a bit later when I saw them on the mantel in the lounge room. At first, I didn't recognise them. They were like little pieces of wood, maybe from the fireplace. I didn't ask what they were doing there, dark purple and turning black. I didn't ask, but I wondered about it.

He wore the shirt on his hand for a while, and his arm swelled up. At night, he'd take the shirt off and squeeze yellow liquid out of where his fingers used to be.

'Pus,' he said. 'That's good. Helps get rid of the infection.'

I could smell it, and it wasn't good, no matter what he said. It smelled like the rabbit and the goat meat smell sometimes.

After a while, his arm and hand started to get better. Then he told me why he put the fingers on the mantel, even though I didn't ask.

'Just a reminder. To be careful.'

After seeing what I saw, I didn't really need a reminder. And the reminder is right there on his hand anyway.

So I don't think it's the real reason. I think he likes having them there, mainly because they were part of him. He couldn't throw them away.

They're so awful looking, but you can't look away from them.

Things are like that sometimes. You can't look away, even when you want to.

three

Today we walked to the big dam.

My father has planted trees there now. He got the trees from up on the hill.

'So the banks stay firm this time. For when it starts raining again.'

He planted the trees so the roots will hold the soil together better, so the walls of the big dam won't slide into the water. That's what he tells me.

But there's no water, because it hasn't rained properly in ages.

I remember when the dam used to be pretty full, and he'd take me swimming when it was hot. He'd tie a rope around my waist, so I wouldn't drown, and get me to paddle my arms through the water. The rope would slide up under my arms when he pulled, and it hurt a bit, but I still liked it.

I wasn't much good at swimming, and my head kept going under, but it was nice being in the water. The feeling on my skin, I mean. It was nice too because he'd laugh a bit. He'd laugh when I went under.

He hasn't laughed as much lately. When it stopped raining he stopped laughing. It might be a coincidence, but I don't think so.

Swimming was something we did just for fun. There aren't many things like that. Not anymore. Nothing we do is just for fun now.

•

The trees aren't growing so well, because there's no rain, but also because of the rabbits. The rabbits come and chew the plants, so they never really get a chance to grow properly into trees. I've never seen them do it, but he reckons it's definitely them.

'It's a double-edged sword,' he said.

I looked that up in the dictionary later, and couldn't find the full meaning. Only part of it.

double-edged
presenting both a danger and an advantage.
(of a knife etc.) having two cutting edges.

I know what a sword is, and what a double-edged one might be like. But I could tell he meant something different, so I waited til later to ask him.

I told him what I found in the dictionary, and he scratched his beard. He does that when he's thinking. Then he said it's the same as a double-edged knife.

'The rabbits coming has two sides. Just like a double-edged sword. Or knife.'

In my mind, all swords have a double edge, but I know what he means. He means the rabbits coming is bad in one way, because they eat the plants, but also good because we can catch them. They're not easy to catch, though. He stopped using the rifle on the rabbits a while back.

'Might need the bullets, so I don't want to waste them.'

To me, shooting the rabbits isn't really a waste. But he must have other things on his mind.

I don't like it so much when he shoots the rabbits anyway. Rabbits are pretty nice, really. They're soft and have long ears and all that. But shooting rabbits is much better than the other way.

'Hasn't rained for ages.'

This is another thing he likes to say. He says it even though we both know it already. He's been saying it more lately, I think.

•

There's three reasons, I think, my father says it hasn't rained for ages.

The first one is because he wants it to rain. He's like that sometimes. He says things haven't happened because he really wants them to. Like he's trying to convince the world it should happen, because it hasn't happened in ages.

But I'm pretty sure the world doesn't work like that. I've tried doing it, and it's never worked for me.

The second reason is because of the crop.

crop
produce of cultivated plants, especially cereals.

That sounds more important than what we've got. Ours is zucchini and carrots and potatoes. The old ones died ages ago, and he's been trying to grow new ones from seeds, apart from the potatoes. You don't have to do a lot for them.

It hasn't been raining enough for anything much to grow lately, but if we get the big dam (the reservoir) full again, we'll be able to water the crop, even when it's not raining.

That's the idea.

But it'll have to rain again for that to work.

The third reason is because of the sheep. I love the sheep. I think he does too, but he would never say anything like that. They mostly drink from the small dam (the dam) nowadays, but that's starting to get a bit low.

Now I think about it, there's probably a fourth reason too – a fourth reason he says it hasn't rained in ages. He's probably worried about us, about whether we'll have enough in the tank for ourselves.

'There's always the creek,' he says.

The creek is outside our farm, past the fence. It's on the side of the hill. But it's almost dry now, anyway.

'Too risky to go there very often.'

'Because of the others?' I said.

'Yep. Anyway, this drought will have to end at some point.'

drought

prolonged absence of rain.

He's probably right.

Last year, it was definitely raining more. The farm was doing better. We had zucchini and silverbeet then, which are vegetables.

I don't like them much, but it was definitely better than having goat on its own.

•

I really hate the other way, but my father reckons there's no other choice.

So we laid two traps, both near the plants. He doesn't let me set them up on my own.

I get to do most things, except the traps and shooting. I don't care much about the traps, but I'd like to do some shooting.

He thinks the rabbits will be back for more. He put one near the plant they'd already had a go at, and the other next to one they haven't touched.

The traps are made from steel and have sharp teeth that snap through bone. He handles them carefully, using his boots on the spring to open the jaws, then setting the part where the rabbit steps. It's called the bridge, but it looks nothing like the bridge in the encyclopedia, more like a steel plate, but it's because words can have different meanings.

It makes things harder, because one word can need a lot of different explanations.

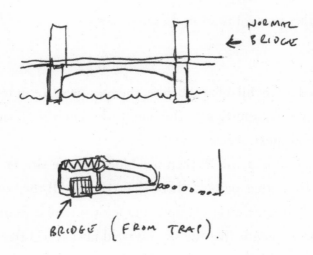

These aren't my best pictures. I might fix them later.

I watched my father put some dry grass over the traps to hide them.

'Rabbits aren't very smart, are they?' I said.

He didn't answer for a bit, put more grass on, then stood up. He shielded his eyes from the sun, put his left hand on his hip. His left hand is the one missing the two fingers. He looked at me, then up at the sky. He breathed in and out deep, like he was thinking about it.

'Suppose they're about as smart as they need to be.' He looked at me funny. 'We can talk about it in the next lesson.'

He didn't really answer my question. He does that sometimes. Answers things in a way that isn't clear, a way that doesn't let things rest. It's annoying, really.

It doesn't give you anything really solid, but makes you think about it even more.

Makes you think of more questions.

•

I started a fire. Like I said before, there's a fireplace in the lounge room, but we mostly use the one in the kitchen. That's where we spend most of our time.

The walls of the kitchen are blue like the sky on a warm day. My mother painted them that colour. All the other walls in the house are creamy white, but a bit yellow in some places.

'She wanted it like the sky, so we'd always feel free.'

That's what he tells me.

Some of the paint is peeling off, and I asked him once if we could fix it. But he never answered.

In the kitchen, there's some old copper saucepans hanging from a rail above the bench. We never use those, but I'm not sure why. Sometimes my father takes them down and cleans them, even though they never get used. The copper frypan is for steak and mushrooms, when we have those, but that isn't very often.

The fire in the kitchen is called a pot-belly. It's black and made of heavy steel, and we use it because he reckons it's more efficient than the fireplace in the lounge room.

I asked him what he meant.

'The wood burns more slowly.'

I looked it up in the dictionary, and it doesn't say anything about firewood. So I reckon that probably isn't true.

efficient

productive with minimum waste or effort.

Efficient is one of those words you can't really draw a picture for. A lot of words are like that. It's easier to draw pictures for things you can see, not so much for words which describe how things work, or how people act. That can be hard to explain.

My mother used to make damper in the pot-belly. That's what my father tells me. Damper is a type of bread, and it's delicious. I know it's delicious because my father made it once for my eighth birthday. He hasn't made it again, even though I've asked him to.

I made us porridge for dinner, which takes a while to cook, but it's really delicious too. I use the porridge pot for the porridge. That's the one pot I'm allowed to use. The porridge pot lives on its own under the bench, not with the copper saucepans or the frypan. Its steel is all black from the heat of the pot-belly, and it isn't as shiny as the copper ones, but I still like it.

Porridge is just oats once they're cooked. He taught me how to make it, and now I have to do it forever. Like most of the jobs around the farm. Except for the traps and the shooting.

The wind got stronger outside and I could feel the cool air on my skin. Even when it's warm in the daytime, the nights are nearly always cold.

I stayed close to the pot-belly, and the heat warmed my bones.

'Why's it called a pot-belly?' I said.

He swallowed down a spoonful of porridge, but a bit stayed on his lip.

'A pot-belly is like a fat belly, like someone who eats too much. So it's because the stove eats a lot of wood. That's why they call it a pot-belly.'

He said before it was more efficient, so that would mean it wouldn't eat lots of wood. But I didn't say anything. It looked like he was in a good mood, so I didn't want to ruin it. Didn't want the soft eyes to come, which has been happening a bit more lately.

They're even worse than when he gets angry. Or just as bad, anyway.

He smiled at me. I saw his gold tooth, which means it's the proper smile. I like the gold tooth. I asked him about it once.

'It's so I can chew things better.'

I don't think that's true, so maybe I'll ask again sometime.

'We should get some wood tomorrow,' he said. 'Maybe in the afternoon, before it gets dark. We'll go on a walk.'

I'm pretty happy about this. I like our walks. He explains things about the farm and the hill on our walks. About the birds and the earth and the sky. More interesting things than our lessons.

I like collecting wood up on the hill too. The hill begins at the end of the paddock, past the fence. I wish we could still use the wheelbarrow, but the tyre broke and he couldn't fix it, even though he tried for ages.

Instead, we carry as much wood as we can in our arms, which is never very much. But it means we get to go there more often, which I like. On the hill, it's always darker and the air is wet and it smells like secrets. I'm looking forward to it.

I've never been to the very top. The top of the hill, I mean. I've asked him plenty of times if I can, and he reckons it's not safe.

'It's always best to stay close to the farm,' he says. 'This is the best place to be.'

But I might ask him again this time. And if he doesn't let me go, I might try to sneak off. He doesn't need to know everything.

It's not got much to do with what happened today, but I can draw a pretty good rabbit. Not perfect, but pretty good. I practise on the blackboard, but my father doesn't know.

I suppose it has got something to do with it, because we set the traps. He did, anyway.

four

I heard voices talking last night.

I've never heard my father talk to someone else. Not that I can remember.

I was in bed, and I heard my father's voice first. He was talking to someone, and then I heard another man with a deep voice.

The man got angry, I could tell, even though I couldn't hear exactly what he was saying.

Then my father said, 'I'd kill you first.'

That was the only thing I heard clearly.

I stayed as quiet as I could. I was scared. The man must've been one of the others. Had to be. I stayed quiet and listened until the talking stopped. After a bit, I must've fallen asleep.

When I got up for breakfast, and to get the fire on, I was a bit scared. I didn't know if the man was still in the house.

I went slowly down the hallway, looked around the corner. There was no one in the kitchen.

After a while, my father's door opened. He came in and did a big stretch with his arms up in the air, just like normal.

The man wasn't in the house – not that I could see, anyway.

I waited til he'd finished his porridge.

'Who were you talking to?'

He looked at me funny.

'What do you mean?'

'I heard you talking last night. To a man. A man with a deep voice.'

He shook his head. 'You must've been dreaming. Or hearing things.'

He frowned, but wouldn't look at me.

But I wasn't dreaming, or hearing things. I definitely heard talking. Two people talking. Him and the man with the deep voice.

But there's not much I can say about it. Not much else without calling him a liar, which I've never done before, even when I know he's definitely not telling the truth.

If I called him a liar, I don't really know how he'd react.

But it wouldn't be good.

I know that for sure.

.

We had a lesson in the school room after breakfast. I use an exercise book for my lessons, which I rest on my lap. It's just like this diary, with lines on the pages so I can keep my writing neat. He reckons that's important.

The encyclopedias are in the school room. They live inside a wooden case. On the wall beside the window that doesn't close properly are two posters. The window doesn't face the hill, like my room does, so I mostly look at the posters.

One has the times-tables, which is part of the maths lessons I don't like doing. The other has the alphabet, with a picture of an animal for each letter. I know both the times-tables and the alphabet without looking at the posters, but I still like looking at the alphabet one.

There's also a framed photo of a man standing at the top of a mountain with his arms up in the air, like he's stretching. It's hanging on the wall above the encyclopedias. The photo has the word 'Achievement' written in big letters underneath, and it has yellow stains where water must have gotten inside the frame.

It was only a short lesson, which is my favourite sort, and it was about different types of sickness. It was about different types of sickness, and what I should do if I have them. He didn't use the blackboard.

We've had a lesson like this before, so he was testing me on what I could remember. My father does that sometimes. It gets boring pretty quick.

'If you have a cold?'

'Rest.'

'A fever?'

'Water.'

'What happens with a fever?'

'You feel cold.'

'And what about a wound?'

'Clean, then bandage it.'

He reckons I need to know these things. Says I need to know in case he isn't around.

Lessons are mostly about practical stuff nowadays, more than maths and words. Things that'll be useful. That's what my father tells me.

He's happy with what I remember, smiles with the gold tooth. He tells me to keep reading the encyclopedias.

•

There's no key for our house or anything. I know about keys though.

My father has shown me the padlock and the key and the chain he keeps in his room, in the cupboard. In the cupboard are tools and things we might need sometimes, but not very often. Like the padlock and the key and the chain.

Keys are used for opening locks, and locks are used for keeping things safe.

It was part of a lesson from ages ago. But I remember.

The medical book is in the cupboard too. The medical book is white and old and I'm not allowed to touch it. He says he used it when my mother got sick, but it didn't work.

I don't remember much about my mother. Only little things, and the things he's told me.

The bendy stick used to live in his cupboard, but not anymore.

•

There's a heavy board we use to lock the house, hung up on two steel brackets. We put it up behind the door whenever we go on a long walk, just to stop the others stealing from us, but it gets jammed sometimes. We only started using it recently, even though no one ever comes. No one except the man with the deep voice, and he's only been once.

My father gave it a shove with his hands, hard against the door.

'Good enough,' he said.

We climbed out the back window, from my bedroom, and dropped to the ground.

I've told him before that if someone came, they could easily go through the window, same way we get out. Especially if they were watching us.

'Maybe,' he said. 'But you'd be surprised how quickly people give up. Just need to make things harder, and sometimes it's enough.'

He could be right.

Don't really know why anyone would come anyway. Only thing they might come for is the rifle.

'Most important thing we've got,' he reckons.

But he always takes it with us anyway, if we're leaving the house and the farm. If we're on one of our walks.

The sun was already high in the sky and I could feel its warmth on my skin. It doesn't take long to walk to the end of the farm, to the fence down there, to where the hill starts. On the outside of the fence, all around, are the trees. They're old and tall and silent, and they don't seem to care if it doesn't rain. They don't seem to care about anything, really.

The sheep watch from the corner of the paddock, down near the dam. They turn their heads toward us, almost all at the same time. A couple are chewing grass, the rest are watching.

I wonder what they're thinking. I wonder if they say to each other, 'There they go, they'll be gone for a while now.'

We're always gone for a while, when we get the wood. Especially since the wheelbarrow broke.

I wonder if sheep act any different when we're not here. Maybe they split up and do their own thing, instead of walking around in a pack. One day, I'll sneak back early and watch, just to check.

He says sheep aren't very smart, and he calls them 'idiots' sometimes, even though I can tell he likes them. But I don't know how he can be sure they're not smart. Just because they don't talk, doesn't mean they're not thinking about things.

The bush doesn't start off thick, and there's a trail which twists right through to where we find the good burning wood. The wood on the ground at the start of the hill isn't that great – it's mostly thin, crackly, and burns up quick. I like it though, especially in the fireplace, which we hardly ever use anymore. We've only used it when it's been really cold, and hardly ever now since the wheelbarrow broke. The fireplace in the lounge room smells like pine cones, and the flames go blue and green. It's really good to watch.

On this walk, he took us further, to where the bush gets thicker. The sweat made a patch between his shoulders, his boots crunching through the twigs. Thin branches scratched at my skin, but that bit doesn't last forever.

The trail gets steeper as we head up the hill. It widens where the gum trees are, and the silver leaves. They're the best for burning, those trees, especially in the pot-belly.

'They burn slow, but throw a lot of heat,' he said.

They have the thicker branches, ones which break and fall in the wind, which is always stronger up the hill.

'Widow makers,' he said. 'That's what people call them.'

He picked up a piece as long as his arm. It was stripped of bark, white and smooth and lovely.

'The branches sometimes fall on people, kill them, so their wife becomes a widow.'

Widow.

It's not a word I've heard before, but it sounds exactly right. It's perfect because the word sounds like what it is.

Some words are like that. *Fluffy* is another one. When I drew my first rabbit, he said it wasn't *fluffy* enough.

I picked up a shorter bit than his, but thicker.

'Should be a good one,' he said.

He smiled at me. Gold tooth.

I was going to ask again about the gold, but I decided to save it for later, for when we're back by the fire and it's night-time. There'll be a story behind it, so it's better to wait for the right moment. Some stories are like that, better to save them up. You don't need to know everything, not all at once.

'Widow,' I say, and I like how it feels in my mouth. The cool air from the hill fills my chest.

'There's also a black widow,' he said, 'which is a spider.'

'Black widow.'

'And a widow's walk.'

He smiled and cracked some branches in his hands. He found a thicker length, its end black like it got burnt a long time ago.

I imagined a widow's walk was a road where the widow goes after someone dies from a tree branch, and it's where they go to walk forever. But I didn't get a chance to say it.

'It's the place on top of the roof of a house. The place where women used to go in the olden days, when their husbands were out at sea. They would look and see if their boat was coming home, which it never was. So it was called the widow's walk.'

It wasn't what I imagined. Not even close. I'm glad I didn't say it to my father.

'Why'd the women do that?' I said. 'Why'd they keep going up there?'

He shrugged.

'How we spend our days is how we spend our lives.'

That's what he said.

I wasn't sure if he was talking about the widows, or maybe their husbands. But I didn't think he'd answer if I asked.

We gathered up as much wood as we could carry. I looked to where the trail went further up the hill. He caught me looking, and I could tell he was thinking about it, because he squinted his eyes.

'We'll go a bit further this time,' he said. 'Let's just leave the wood here.'

•

It was all pretty much the same as where we were. Only difference was the trail got steeper, then opened out a little, like a clearing. We'd been there plenty of times, so it wasn't that exciting.

'Turn around,' he said.

I could see over the trees to where we were before, and down to the farm. I could see the roof of our house and it looked small and dark and square. I only knew where to look because I knew it was there.

Around the farm is thick bush. There's bush as far as you can see, all the way to the sky. But the trees look different from up on the hill. They look green, then blue, and get darker the closer they get to the sky, which is the opposite of what you'd expect. Near the sky is more hills, and I can never see any other farms except ours. I can't see the town, because it's over the other side of the hill. That's what my father tells me.

I couldn't see the sheep, which was a shame because it would have been perfect if I could. Would have been able to see exactly what they were doing, and they wouldn't have seen us.

Maybe they were doing something really unexpected this time. Maybe they'd gone in the house and were sitting around and talking and eating porridge. But the door was locked, so there's no way that could be true. Unless they watched us and went through the window.

'Can we go a bit higher?' I said.

My father looked at me, his face suddenly dark from the shadow of the trees. I hoped he'd smile and I'd see the gold tooth. And he'd say yes.

His left eye twitched. He scratched his beard, then shook his head.

We headed back down the hill, but I've decided I'll go up further another time. When he isn't around. I've done it before, but he doesn't know.

Like I said, he doesn't need to know everything.

five

We saw my mother on the way back.

She's not on the farm, she's in the bush. Off the main track, about half-way down from where we get the wood.

I didn't really feel like going. It's not because I don't care, but because the wood was heavy, and because I wanted to see what the sheep were doing.

But I couldn't say so.

It's hard to care so much, because she was gone before I could ever really know her. I'd never say that out loud, and definitely not to him. And it's not her fault, because it's been me and him pretty much the whole time.

I remember some things, though. Some things about her. I think I do.

I remember how she used to smooth my hair. I'd be sitting on the floor by the fire, between her knees, and she'd smooth my hair with her hands, especially if I was upset.

I liked the feeling. I remember feeling warm and safe by the fire. I liked the feeling of being close to her.

Be brave.

That's what she said. I told him about it once, and he didn't remember her ever saying that. He said maybe it happened, but it could be my imagination.

But why would I remember those words so clearly, if she never said them?

I remember some other things too. Other things I haven't told him. Things I didn't like so much.

Like hearing her crying.

I remember that. The feeling of it. I don't think it's my imagination. Same with the other thing. But I never ask him about the crying.

There's probably a word for when a child is a widow, when they lose their mother. Or their father. Or both.

Maybe I'll ask him.

It'd be good if there was some kind of reverse dictionary, where I could look up the meanings to find out what the word is.

I don't have a photo of my mother. I only have a picture of her in my mind. She had black hair, curly, a big smile, and pale skin. There's a woman in one of the magazines that looks a bit like my mother. It's in one of her old magazines, the *Women's Weekly*.

Her name is Elizabeth Taylor, the woman in the photo. She has dark shiny eyes, white teeth, and bright red lips.

I don't know my mother's name. I don't think it matters so much. You're not supposed to call your mother or father by their names. Not sure why, but he told me that once.

I'd like to know, though. What her name is.

•

It's not a normal grave. I looked that up in the dictionary ages ago, and it didn't sound like her one.

grave

trench dug in the ground for the burial of a corpse; mound
or memorial stone placed over this.

My mother's hasn't got a stone or a trench. It's just dirt with a star picket at one end. My father put the picket in when he buried her, so he'd know where to find it. That's what he tells me.

When we go see my mother, he sometimes puts things on the picket, like an old shirt, or some flowers he's picked. But the flowers mostly only happen when it's warm.

I found a picture of a grave in the encyclopedia. The one in the encyclopedia looks like this.

That's my copy of it. I didn't trace it.

Her one is a bit different. It looks like this.

He's always quiet when we're there. Both of us are. But the last time we were there, he said something.

He said, 'No one can choose how they leave this earth.'

I've been thinking about that, what he meant by it, but I haven't asked him about it.

There was only one other time he said something. It was a long time ago. He said it to her, not to me.

'Maybe you were right.'

He said it so soft, I barely heard it. But I've never forgotten it. I wondered what he meant, and what she was right about. But I've never asked.

He didn't say anything this time, or put anything on the picket. He just stood there, eyes closed, for ages. I kept quiet, stared at the picket. I was bored as anything, if I'm honest. I tried for a bit to think about Elizabeth Taylor. I tried to make myself upset. It didn't work.

I think it's because I was still thinking about the sheep, wondering what they were doing. And maybe the gold tooth. Those two things.

There's usually a maximum of three things I can keep in my mind at once. Sometimes just two.

•

I tried to go slow when we got to the edge of the bush, so the sheep wouldn't hear and I'd catch them in the act. Because they probably weren't in the house, I decided they might be walking around on their back legs, pretending to be people. Maybe they were pretending to be me and him, making fun of us, repeating things we say and having a laugh about it.

Not sure he'd find it funny, though. I could tell from his mood since he saw my mother. The way he'd stayed quiet.

He was walking ahead of me and making too much noise, but I couldn't tell him to stop. Then I'd have to explain everything I was thinking.

I could smell his salty sweat from the sun and see the dark spots under his arms. I stayed quiet.

He gets in a funny mood after he goes to see her. Sometimes, he gets the soft eyes. If he gets the soft eyes, I don't see the gold tooth for days.

When he gets the soft eyes, it's like he's not really looking at anything. It's like he's looking at something inside of himself, or something from the past. It's hard to explain. And it's been happening more than it used to. It scares me, and I'm not sure why.

I wonder sometimes if he used to get the soft eyes when my mother was here. I can't remember, but I doubt it.

When he gets them, he acts different. He doesn't talk much. And when he does talk, his voice is slower and harder to hear.

When he's like that, he doesn't answer my questions. Even less than normal. There's no point in asking. He stops looking at me. But then I catch him staring sometimes, when he thinks I can't see.

·

The sheep were in a different spot than when we left, but in a group like they normally are. They were up in the corner of the farm, closer to the house. It made me think they might've tried to get in the house, through the window, but I can't prove it. I don't have any *evidence*, which is a word we talked about the other day in a lesson.

evidence
*available facts, circumstances etc. indicating whether or not
    a thing is true or valid.*

Here's a picture of a widow's walk, just while I think of it. Might not be exactly what it looks like, but I'm going by what he explained to me. There's no widow's walk in the dictionary, or in the encyclopedia. And there isn't one on our roof.

One day, when I'm grown up, I'll check the real-life versions of these pictures, just to see if I've got them right. But I'll have to leave the farm to do it.

'When you're older,' he says.

That's when I can leave if I want, but I'd have to risk it with the others. That's what my father tells me.

Here's a picture of a black widow, which is the spider he was talking about. Don't know if this is exactly right, but most spiders look the same.

•

It was nearly dark by the time we got back. The sun always goes down over the hill, so it gets darker for us much sooner than the others. That's what my father tells me.

Before we went in, he got a rabbit from the pit. He mustn't have checked the traps yet. The pit is where we keep the meat, wrapped in wet hessian, so it keeps cooler and won't rot as quick.

We keep goat meat there too, when we have that. Sometimes it's gone green if the weather's warm, but he normally cuts those bits out. When he opens the pit, the smell always comes out. It doesn't matter where I am in the house, I can smell it.

I was glad he got a rabbit, because the night before I cooked porridge for dinner, and even though porridge is delicious, you can get sick of it. And I get sick of cooking it sometimes.

I looked back to the hill and thought about the others.

'If the others come, everything will change.'

That's what he says sometimes.

Don't really know much about what they're like. Don't know how they look, or anything else about them. I reckon he prefers it like that. My mother would know, but she's dead.

•

He cooked it good this time. He always cooks the meat and I do the porridge. That's the deal. He served it up and it was nicer, with the crispy bits, and the meat cooked right through. He cooked it on top of the pot-belly, and the fire was hot, and I liked listening to the sizzle in the pan. There was no bits of fur in it, which happens sometimes if you don't skin it properly.

Skinning the rabbits is the worst bit. Gutting them too. But I'm getting better at it.

It was a good one this time, and not too tough. The only problem with rabbits is they're really bony, so you have to be careful the bones don't stick in your throat and choke you.

Rabbit can be chewy sometimes too, if they're old, or if they got a lot of exercise. This one was just right.

After we ate, I asked about whether he was a widow. I asked him after we finished the rabbit. But before I asked about the widow, he talked about the lamb.

He looked me right in the eyes. He usually does that when he says something that'll make me upset. Like when he tells me off for not watering the crop properly. Or if I'm asking too many questions about things. Or if I make mistakes in the lessons.

'We might cook one,' he said.

I used to think he looked at me like that because he wanted me to be upset, like he enjoyed it, but now I think it's something different.

'Okay,' I said.

It was the opposite of what I was thinking, what I was feeling. But I was trying to be tough about it.

I tried not to think about the lamb, who isn't born yet. I tried not to think about its eyes and its wool and its tail. I tried not to think of its mother and how she would be calling out. She'll be calling out when he does it. When he slaughters the lamb with his knife. That's always how he does it.

Truth is, I like the taste of lamb. But I like them much better alive.

I could feel his eyes on me, so I concentrated hard on the bones of the rabbit, but then it became the lamb.

'Are you a widow?' I said.

I said it because I wanted him to stop looking at me. And I wanted to stop thinking about the lamb.

He coughed. Crossed one arm under the other. The pot-belly stove cracked from the heat. It does that sometimes.

'Widower,' he said. 'It's the male version of a widow.'

Widower.

I liked the sound of it. It sounded even better than widow, more lonely. I said it out loud and it felt good in my mouth, and it helped me stop thinking about the lamb. Pushed it out. Only room for one thing this time.

'Widower.'

'Yep.'

'How did it happen?'

'What happen?'

'My mother. How did she die?'

I was trying to make him forget about the lamb.

He breathed in very deep.

'You know what happened. She got sick. And she wouldn't listen.'

He leaned over, took my plate.

And I knew he wasn't going to say anything else about it.

•

When she got sick, it was pretty terrible. I remember bits of it.

I think I do.

I remember how she was in bed for a long time. She didn't come out of their bedroom, and I wasn't allowed in.

I remember him going in there. And I remember him reading the old white medical book at the kitchen table.

I remember her crying. The sound from their room.

These are the things I remember. I think I do.

I kind of wish I hadn't brought it up. I hope he doesn't get the soft eyes.

He rinsed the plates in the bucket. I took another piece of wood, a thick one, and opened the pot-belly. It was the wood I'd found. The pot-belly was red and hot and flaming inside, and the heat hit my cheeks.

I liked the feeling.

The wood didn't catch straight away. I closed the pot-belly and pulled my chair up close.

He sat down and got close to the fire too. He showed me the gold tooth, rubbed my shoulder. He stretched his legs out and closed his eyes, but he wasn't sleeping.

I'd draw a picture of his face, but it's too hard. Faces are complicated. They change too much. His especially.

I'll try to draw a widower instead, like the woman on the widow's walk, but a man.

It's not as good as the other picture.

A widower might not act like a widow anyway. Maybe a widower would just go on with his life, kill a lamb for dinner. Smile with the gold tooth.

The Others

I'm trying not to think too much about what he said. It'll be a little while yet. He'll change his mind, or forget. He does that sometimes.

six

There's a race we have sometimes. A running race. It's from the house, down to the dam, then back again.

The sheep look at us like we're crazy. I think they wonder why we're running, or maybe wonder what we're running from.

I used to beat my father every time, but then I realised he was going slow on purpose. So I made him run properly. He said because I was still young, he was just trying to make it fair.

Since he started running properly, he's won every time. But I've been getting close. The last few times, I got close enough to hear his breaths and smell his sweat. Close enough that he stopped laughing, and I could tell he was really trying.

I don't think he wanted me to beat him.

There's no prize for winning. He said that in running, there's sometimes a prize, like a medal or a trophy. But there's no prize when we run.

'Just the glory,' he said. I could see his gold tooth.

But we haven't had a race for ages. At first, I thought it was because he was worried I would beat him.

But when I asked, he said, 'Don't fucking nag me!'

I saw the whites of his eyes.

So I haven't asked again.

Not since he said that.

I think it's because of the drought. I think he's worried about it not raining, and it's making things worse. It's making him get angry real quick.

Or maybe he's worried about the man with the deep voice.

About the others.

·

My father has never explained, not completely, who the others are. And I can tell he doesn't like talking about it. But I know a bit from what I've asked, from what he's told me.

They live over the hill, and only come out when it's dark.

In the house, at night, I mostly feel safe. Sometimes I hear noises like the fence creaking, wires bending – sometimes I think the others are coming, coming right up to the house.

I close my eyes and try to listen.

I wonder whether to wake him, so he can get the rifle. He keeps it under his bed.

But the noise always stops, eventually.

When I tell him in the morning, he reckons it was my imagination.

'Must have been the wind,' he says. 'Your ears playing tricks on you.'

So I don't tell him so much anymore. I keep it to myself.

Some of the others are from the commune. The commune is where my father and my mother went after the town, the place he doesn't like talking about very much. He says people in the town had the plague, so they had to leave. The commune was like the town, only smaller.

But things went wrong at the commune. And he says some of the people there got the plague too.

He and my mother used to talk about the commune. I can't remember them talking about it, but he's told me. He told me they had to leave.

He said he didn't like their vision at the commune, but my mother disagreed.

vision
imaginative planning for the future.

There are a lot of different meanings for that word, but I worked it out eventually. That's the right one, I think. Or this one.

It's definitely one of these two.

vision
thing or person seen in a dream or trance.

Probably the first one.

With the others, I worry about the sheep mostly, because they're out there on their own. I worry the others could come and take them away.

They're always the first thing I look for in the morning. I open the door and check the sheep are still there. I'm not allowed out too much on my own. Mostly just with my father, when we're working on the farm, or getting wood.

He doesn't like me out on my own, just in case the others see me.

•

This morning, they were down near the dam again. The sheep, I mean. The sun wasn't up completely, so it was cold, and they were bunched tight together. I closed the door and went to the pot-belly. It was still burning a bit from last night, so I put some paper inside and tried to get it going.

I could hear him snoring. It was just light outside, so I tried to be as quiet as I could. Once the flame picked up, I lit one of the candles.

I went back to my bedroom and got the *Women's Weekly* out from under the bed. I look after it properly, because paper doesn't last forever. It doesn't stay perfect, especially in the sunlight. Hopefully this diary does, or at least for a while.

I keep the *Women's Weekly* under the bed because I'm worried he'll use it on the fire, and then Elizabeth Taylor will be gone forever. She'll only be in my mind, and she won't stay there, not clearly.

I tried once not looking at it for a while, then tried to remember what she looked like, things like the colour of her eyes and the shape of her lips. When I looked at the real photo, it was different. I'd gotten it wrong.

Your mind can play tricks on you, like your ears, so you need to look after things like that – the things that remind you. You need to keep them safe.

In the *Women's Weekly*, I found someone named Larry Hagman.

He could be one.

Someone from the commune. Someone with the plague.

It says he's from Dallas, which could be where they live now. But he doesn't look mean enough, I think, to be one of the others. He should have sharp teeth or something.

The problem with Larry Hagman is that I can only really trace his hat through the paper, so I have to do the rest myself.

This is what he looks like.

•

After breakfast, we went out to check on the sheep. They all moved away from me, but not too far. I counted them. Twelve exactly. Two smaller ones, that were born last spring. They're not fully grown yet, but close.

David and Charlene.

David was named after David Hasselhoff, who's like a superhero, and he drives a black car named Kitt. He's from one of the pages that's faded in the *Women's Weekly*, because my mother must have left it out in the sun. The other one is named Charlene, and she's also named Kylie Minogue.

After I named them, my father told me David was actually a girl. The sheep, I mean, not the one in the *Women's Weekly*. I was going to change her name, but my father said it doesn't matter.

I haven't named the older sheep, but I know which one is which. There's one who's a ram, because he's got horns that curl, and I stay away from him. He's called the old bastard, but it's not his real name. There's the two who'll have lambs, because they're all swollen up. The old bastard is the father.

I wonder what would happen if I set them free, the swollen ones. If I made a gap in the fence and let them out. Nothing would happen to the lambs then.

But seeing how sheep usually behave, I don't think they would go anyway. They always stick together, in a pack. And I'd probably never do it, if I'm honest.

There's still time. I'll convince him not to eat the lambs, that it's better if we keep them. I might write a list. A list of reasons not to eat them.

If my mother was still here, he wouldn't do it. I don't know that for sure, but it's just a feeling. It'd be two against one.

One time, when I was younger, we had porridge with milk. It was milk from the sheep, and my mother made it, and it was delicious. It was on my birthday, because when I asked him about it once, he said he remembered it too. He didn't say it was my imagination.

He reckons the milk is just for special occasions, like my birthday. There hasn't been another day as good as that for ages.

I'll remind him about the milk in the porridge and how good it tasted, and that we need the wool too. These are things to put on my list.

That's the main thing with the sheep – to help keep the farm going, so he doesn't have to go into town anymore. Because we'll have milk and meat for food, and wool for clothes and blankets like the green one. Plus the crop.

They smell a bit, the sheep. But not in a bad way. Not like the goat meat. And I like the noises they make, and the feel of their wool. Kind of oily, but soft too. They always feel warm, even when it's cold. I like how they bunch up close, especially when there's bad weather, like they're all in it together. They never let anyone stand out on their own.

'It's instinct,' he says.

Instinct.

He told me that means it comes naturally, without them even thinking about it. I still think it's pretty good. In some ways, it's probably even better they're not thinking about it. It's not because they expect something in return.

After we checked on the sheep, he started moving old sheets of tin near the house. I stayed with the sheep. He was being noisy, but it took a while for the noise to come to my ears. He threw a sheet of tin on top of another sheet, but it was a second or two until I heard it.

The others are further away, so it would take even longer for them to hear something like that. In the commune. Or maybe in Dallas.

I looked up to the hill, all thick bush and grey-green. I couldn't see the trail from there, but I wondered how long it goes for, and if it goes all the way to Dallas.

But I saw something else. I saw something up near the top of the hill, sliding like a dark snake into the pale blue sky. I saw it, and it looked exactly like this.

This is exactly what it looked like.

seven

We go in buckets. Both of us have our own, made from steel, and they're mostly kept outside, except at night. They're different from the watering buckets – we always keep those ones separate.

We empty them in the sewer, but not at the same time. That'd be disgusting. In the olden days, he says that's how they would have done it anyway, in buckets, so we shouldn't be too precious about it.

Had to look up that word, *precious*, because I thought it meant something different.

precious
of great value or worth.

It did mean what I thought. So maybe he meant we shouldn't think we're too special, or valuable, to be doing it in buckets.

The sewer is a fair way from the house, and it's just a deep hole in the ground. Doesn't sound like the sewer in the dictionary, even if he calls it that.

sewer

conduit, usu. underground, for carrying off drainage water and sewage.

He says it was probably once a mineshaft, or an old well. A mineshaft is what they used to find gold, which was used to make jewellery and things like that. Yellow and shiny. There's pictures of it in the encyclopedia, like the gold in his tooth. Haven't asked him about that again, because it doesn't seem as important anymore.

Things are like that sometimes.

A well is what was used for water before water tanks. I think it's more likely it was a mineshaft.

Well is another word with more than one meaning. There's so many like that.

Whatever the hole was, it's disgusting now. I keep away from it, apart from when I have to empty the bucket, which is one of the worst jobs there is.

That's all I want to write about it.

•

For breakfast we always have porridge, and it's good because it warms you up a bit.

The day after I saw the snake in the sky, I overcooked the oats. I wasn't paying attention and there was some hard, black bits in them. It came out bitter. He finished before me, put his bowl in the bucket.

We don't talk much during breakfast. It's always been like that.

After breakfast, we had a lesson in the school room. We had a lesson which was maths, which is one of my least favourite. I definitely prefer the ones with reading and writing, or the practical ones. The ones about words are better.

We did the times-tables, which are on the poster near the window. He made me face away from the poster, and close my eyes, so I couldn't see the answers. Thing is, I only ever did that once, ages ago, and he belted me for it with the bendy stick. I haven't done it again since.

We did the seven times-tables, which I've had trouble with before. He says I need to learn these things, but they're confusing sometimes. I got them right this time, though. I got them all the way to eighty-four.

'Good boy,' he said.

He stood up and dusted his hands on his pants. His pants are green and nearly always dirty.

'Let's go clean up the plates,' he said. 'Then I'll go check the traps.'

He stood there, looking at me. He's much taller than me, but reckons I still have a long time to grow.

'So?' he said.

I knew what he was waiting for. He was waiting for me to ask a question, because I always ask a question at the end of a lesson.

It's because nearly every night, before I go to sleep, I read something from the encyclopedia. Most mornings, I need to ask about it, but I always wait until the end of our lessons.

But lately, I haven't been reading the encyclopedia so much. Mainly because I've been writing in this diary, which is what he told me to do.

This time, I wasn't sure he'd know the answer anyway. That's only happened a couple of times, like when I asked something about outer space. He got the soft eyes afterwards, which might have been a coincidence, but just in case it wasn't, I decided not to ask about things like that again. The things that don't have just one answer. Things that are complicated. Like the commune. Things like that.

But I could tell I had to ask something.

'Who wrote the encyclopedia?'

He frowned.

'Why?'

'Just curious.'

He shifted his weight from one leg to the other, like maybe that would help. Help him get to the right answer.

'Well, people who knew everything. Professors. People like that.'

I could tell he wasn't really sure, because his gaze drifted up toward the ceiling, like he thought the right answer might be somewhere up there.

So I decided to ask what I really wanted to ask.

'What about the others?'

He crossed his arms.

'The others?'

'Yeah. How come they're not in there? I mean, if the people who wrote it knew everything?'

He smiled a little, but no gold tooth. Just the corner of his mouth. He smiled in the way he does sometimes, when I've got the wrong end of the stick. That's something he says, which I've never really understood either. But I didn't want to say I didn't understand it, after already not understanding something, if you know what I mean.

'They came after,' he said. 'After it was written.'

I suppose that makes sense.

'Where did they come from?' I said.

'From over the hill.'

'From the commune?'

'Some of them. I've already told you about it. Anyway, those dishes won't clean themselves.'

I followed him to the kitchen.

'When did they come?' I said.

'Who?'

'The others.'

'After the encyclopedia was written. Anyway, that's enough fucking questions, isn't it?'

I saw the whites of his eyes, and I knew not to answer.

'I've already told you what happened, more than once.'

And I know, he has already told me. He told me it was after everything changed. It was after the plague. The plague was a disease and nearly everyone died.

Except the others.

I wonder if the smoke snake was in the sky when they came. If my mother was here, I'd ask her, but she's dead.

I can't ask him anything else. Not at the moment. There's something about his eyes which is making me nervous, more than normal. His body too. It's like he's gone all stiff inside. I can feel it inside of me too, like I've caught it from him.

I have to wait for the right time.

•

I watched him through the window, and he came back from the traps with nothing. He stopped before the house, lifting sheets of tin, flipping them over. There's lots of sheets of tin and iron around the place, mostly rusted. They've always been here. We use them to patch things up on the house sometimes. I hold the sheets, and he screws them in.

I went out to him.

He crouched down and picked up the edge of a long, battered sheet of corrugated iron. It was rusty, half sunk into the earth.

I've never liked touching the sheets that much. There's spiders sometimes. Could be black widows.

'Watch this,' he said.

He stood up quick, flipped the iron over. Dust went everywhere, up my nose, and in my throat.

Mice, lots of them, in all directions.

'Mice,' he said, as if I didn't see.

They ran off into the long yellow grass.

'Bit of a problem,' he said.

He chewed his bottom lip, hands on hips. The two missing fingers, both inside on the mantel. I wonder if he misses them.

He passed me a star picket. Same as the ones he uses for the plants near the big dam. Same as my mother's grave, but shorter.

'It's a good job for you,' he said. 'Keep you busy. For the next few days, anyway.'

I wonder if I should tell him about the smoke snake. I looked at the hill today but didn't see anything. I stared hard, into a wisp of cloud, and wondered if that was it.

Your mind can play tricks on you sometimes. Same as with your ears. And your eyes.

Best not to say anything.

•

It wasn't a good job for me. Almost as bad as the sewer.

I lifted the sheets of tin and iron, and nearly all of them had mice underneath. The only ones I could get with the picket were the baby ones, because they were slow. Or some bigger ones, who were probably sick.

Either way, it was pretty disgusting – their guts burst out, heads popped, but there wasn't much blood. Probably pretty useless anyway. For every one I killed, most of them got away.

But I do what he asks me, even if I don't like it. Same with watering the crop. I do these things mainly because I don't want him to get the soft eyes. When the soft eyes come, he doesn't talk very much. Doesn't talk and stays in bed for ages.

The soft eyes are worse than when he gets angry. They hang around like the fog. Like the fog on the hill in winter. That's what it's like. But when he gets angry, even if the whites of his eyes scare me, it passes pretty quick. It's more like a storm coming over the hill. A storm in spring. Raining hard, then passing. Different from the fog.

Like I said, I don't think he would've got the soft eyes when my mother was here. Not as much.

Maybe it's because she's gone, and because of the drought too. Both these things.

The other job he gave me was to clean the oats, to pick out the little black droppings. It was almost as bad as killing the mice. But he reckoned it was important, because we can't afford to waste any food.

He watched me when I was doing it, which made me think he should probably just do it himself. But I didn't say so.

'Might have to go hunting tomorrow,' he said. 'You can keep going with it then.'

But I've decided, just to myself, that when he goes, I'll go up the hill. I know I'm supposed to stay in my room, but he won't know. Might check if I can see anything. Just to make sure about the smoke, or the cloud, or whatever it was.

He doesn't need to know about it.

Not yet.

eight

My father left when the sun was still climbing, early in the day. He always leaves early, never late. So he's back before dark. Before the others.

I watched him head toward the hill, the rifle slung across his back, knife in his belt. The trees took him in.

I waited.

Sometimes, he comes back quick. Like if he's forgotten something, usually his hessian sack. Sometimes, he does it deliberately, I think, to check on me. It's a trick. To see if I stay in my room.

So I got the encyclopedia out from the school room. I'm up to F, and there's something about *famine*, which has pictures of skinny people with round bellies and flies in their mouths. I can't understand all the words, but figured out some of it. A lot of people died in the 1980s because there wasn't enough food.

The next one was about something called *fascism*, and I can't really understand much about that. There's a picture of a man in a uniform and a hat, with people watching him. The photo is black-and-white, so must be from the olden days. There's another photo too, which is pretty awful. Bones and skeletons all piled up.

The word *politics* is in there a few times.

My father has said that word before too, mainly when he's talking about things that happened in the commune, and also about what happened at the town. Mostly about the commune. Sometimes he says, 'Fucking politics,' or 'The politics were all bullshit.'

I never really understood when he explained it, and not even the dictionary helps.

politics
art and science of government.

He usually gets fired up when he talks about it. His face goes red, and I see the whites of his eyes sometimes. To be honest, I'm not really that interested in it. I don't like it when he's angry.

•

I thought he'd been gone long enough.

I went out of the house and across the paddock. The wind was coming down from the hill, and the air was cool. The sheep all looked at me from the small dam, and I felt a stab in my belly like I didn't want them to see, like I was doing something wrong. But I wasn't, not really. I was just checking on what I saw.

Just to be sure. To be careful. That's what I told myself.

I knew if he caught me, it wouldn't be good. The bendy stick could come back.

Before I got to the fence, I could already smell it. The wind was bringing it to me. It was definitely smoke, or fire, but I couldn't see anything. I know exactly what it smells like, because of the pot-belly.

I looked up to the sky, but there was nothing. The wind could be different up there, could be blowing the smoke snake the other way, away from the farm and over the hill. Maybe to Dallas. To the commune. To where the others are.

Maybe the others are out there, waiting for him.

My chest thumped hard. I climbed between the wires and started walking up the trail, through the bush.

The smell was getting stronger. Like earth and smoke and something sweet.

I stopped where the trail turned off to where my mother is, to catch my breath. It's always darker on the hill than on the farm, and I'm definitely not supposed to be there on my own. 'Never,' he says.

The wind blew hard and the smell of smoke got stronger, in my nose and mouth, bitter on my tongue.

Crack!

A gunshot.

I stopped breathing, stood still. I listened, listened for anything else. But it's all I heard. And it's all I normally hear – one shot.

He must've got one.

I guessed he'd be a little while, because he'd have to do the slaughtering, fill his hessian sack. The blood soaking through and onto his back when he carries what he can back to the house. Before the sun goes down and the moon and the others come out.

I knew he'd be a little while yet, but not too long.

I headed back down the trail.

Past the spot where my mother is.

Back to the farm.

I'll tell him after.

•

He's more careful when he cuts the meat. More careful, I think, since he lost his fingers.

He cuts the skin off first, then slowly through the flesh. It didn't look as bloody as usual, some of it must have dripped out on the way down. The back of his shirt and pants were soaked deep red, and I wished he'd change them. The smell was making me feel sick.

'I saw smoke,' I said.

The words felt strange in my mouth, but sounded even worse once they were out. I wished I could reach into the space between us, before they got to his ears, and pull them back in.

He kept cutting, didn't look up.

I'd started, so there was no stopping.

'Smoke. Up on the hill. I saw it, and I could smell it too.'

I watched him close, he didn't react. Pink-white bone and his blade. Tendons, veins. Blood pooled on the bench.

'Smoke?' he said.

'Yep.'

He shrugged, wiped his hands on his shirt. Eyed me.

'How'd you see that?'

'From my room. Through the window.'

It wasn't the truth, not completely. He doesn't need to know everything.

'The fire,' he said.

He nodded toward the pot-belly.

'The fire was out,' I said.

He flipped the meat over. It looked like it might be a thigh. Thick and muscly, with long, pink streams of flesh.

I prefer the rabbit than the goat, definitely. The goat has a really strong smell, especially when he roasts it. If he has smaller pieces, and can fry it, that's usually better. But the roast really stinks out the house. And we're usually eating it for days, especially if the weather's cool, and it takes ages to go rotten.

The goat meat is grey and chewy, and full of nervy bits. Tendons, he calls them. When he chews, I hear them crunch in his teeth.

When it goes off, it's a bit green first, then darker. Sometimes, he cooks it when it's green. That's really the worst.

'Might roast this one,' he said. 'Could be a bit tough.'

I could tell he didn't want to talk about it, about the smoke. Same as when I ask about the commune. Or the town. Or how things were before. Or the others.

All these things.

'I saw it. Definitely. Up on the hill,' I said.

'You're probably imagining it. Could even be mist, from the bush. Or a bit of fog.'

I knew it was too early for fog, but I didn't say anything.

'What about the others?' I said.

He plunged his right hand into the meat, through the muscle, and gripped the bone. The meat squelched and thick blood oozed out onto the bench – he pulled the bone hard, but it wouldn't come free.

He took the knife again and made fresh, deeper cuts.

'Nah,' he said. 'Only out at night, remember?'

He concentrated on the meat.

'What if they've changed things? What if they're coming closer?'

He shook his head. 'They sleep during the day. They're parasites. Like vampires.'

He gripped the knob at the end of the bone, pulled it free. He smiled, gold tooth. Held the bone up like a prize.

'Vampires?'

He stopped smiling. No gold tooth.

'Look, it's good you're keeping an eye out. But there's no need to worry.'

He reckoned I should concentrate on my job instead.

'The mice are still getting into the oats.'

Don't think there's much point me going around and hitting the mice with the picket. If anything, it might be making things worse. They'll realise it's not safe for them, under the tin and the iron, and they'll come into the house.

But I didn't say anything.

I don't like doing it, but I'll keep doing it for him. Think he knows it too, which is why I don't say anything. Sometimes, he knows without me saying.

He says we need to look after the oats, because the crop still isn't doing very good.

'We're definitely in a drought this time, a long one.'

Just while I think of it, this is what a mouse looks like.

It's not as good as my rabbit picture, but not bad.

I think he already knew about the smoke. I don't know for sure, but I got a feeling.

I can't explain exactly why, but I could tell.

•

The encyclopedia has one page about vampires, but no pictures.

I can understand some of it, about a book by someone called Bram Stoker, and something about animals called bats, who have wings like birds.

It says vampires are *supernatural*, and I had to look that word up in the dictionary.

supernatural
not attributable to, or explicable by, the laws of nature.

The encyclopedia also talks about a disease called *syphilis*, which is impossible to say properly out loud. Same as *fascism* – my tongue gets twisted. And I'm not sure what it's got to do with the others anyway.

It says they drink blood and have sharp teeth. Other thing is, they're not real. They're make-believe. So I wonder why he said the others are like that.

I'll try to draw one. I'll try to draw a vampire, as if they were one of the others. The encyclopedia said vampires sleep in something called a *coffin*. Like they're dead.

coffin
box in which a corpse is buried or cremated.

So it's like they're alive and dead at the same time, which I don't completely understand. Not at all, if I'm honest.

But they're not real anyway.

Makes me wonder if my mother is in a coffin too.

It's something I don't like thinking about much, and I can't remember if she was, but I wrote it down now to get it out of my thoughts.

It's funny how sometimes writing things down can do that. Not always, but sometimes.

nine

W̲e catch yabbies in the dam sometimes.
It's pretty great.

yabby
freshwater crayfish valued as food.

It isn't easy to catch them. We use bits of goat that have gone off, and tie them to pieces of string. We sit there for ages, and wait for the string to go tight, which means a yabby is on the end of it. You have to pull them up quick, then scoop them out from underneath. It's tricky, because yabbies have claws and they hurt like anything if they get hold of you.

This is what they look like. More or less.

Once we get a few, we cook them in a pot of water until their shells go bright red. They're really delicious. The tail is the nicest bit, with the most flesh, but the claws are good too.

On my ninth birthday, we caught yabbies and had them for dinner. My father gave me all the tails, and it was one of the best birthdays I can remember. I tried to share some with him, but he said they were all for me. He said it was a special treat, and that it's important to have a treat every now and then.

That's what my father told me.

He eats the head and the eyes and the guts and everything, but I tried that once and it was bitter and disgusting. He thought my face was pretty funny. He laughed and it almost made me feel like it was worth it.

Me and him usually have a competition to see who gets the most. Who catches the most yabbies, I mean. It's pretty close most times, but I usually win, even if he has to help me a bit. His hands are bigger, so it's easier for him to scoop them up out of the water.

But we haven't done it in ages. Yabbying, I mean. I asked him why a while back, and he said it's because of the drought.

'Dam's too low now,' he said. 'We don't want to lose them altogether.'

I wanted to ask what he meant, but he wasn't in a good mood. I figured it out myself later on.

If we take too many yabbies, then there won't be enough left, and they won't be able to breed. Especially if there isn't much water.

I understand what he means, but I still miss doing it.

That's the thing about things that are good. It always seems like they never last. But bad things, they can go on forever.

ten

Something happened. One of the sheep.
She was flat on the ground, and you hardly ever see that with the sheep. They sleep like that sometimes, but not very often. They usually only lie down when they're sick. The old bastard got sick a while back, but he came good.

When I saw her on the ground, I asked him.

'Is she okay?'

He smiled. Gold tooth.

'The lamb decides the time, not the ewe.'

That's what he said.

ewe
female sheep.

It sounds the same as *you*. It's one of those words.

She looked worried, so I crouched down beside her and rubbed her head, her soft ears. The other sheep were around, but not as close as usual. Like they were nervous. Keeping their distance.

Her breaths puffed in and out fast. I looked into her eyes, their funny shape. Not the eye itself, but the middle of it. The middle part isn't round like our eyes, but kind of square, rectangle.

It might look scary if you didn't know how gentle they are.

He had gumboots on, but I thought that was way over the top.

'Have a look,' he said.

I stood up and went around the back of the sheep, where he was. I've seen it happen before, and it's all pretty disgusting. This time, there was a big pink bubble coming out of her bum.

He saw my face and laughed. First time in ages.

'The water bag,' he said.

We watched it get bigger, then it broke. His boots got a spray. I still thought it was over the top, wearing the gumboots, I mean.

I wondered why he needed to stand so close. And I wondered why he had the knife in his belt.

'Just making sure everything's okay.'

It was like he could see my thoughts, see them through my eyes.

'Look.' He pointed.

And then I saw it, the tip of the nose, then its feet. The ewe let out a long groan, and the other sheep shuffled backwards into each other, into the fence. They all watched sideways, and I watched them because it was better than looking at the ewe.

She called out again and the lamb got pushed out proper this time, all bloody and wet. You wouldn't recognise it straight away, that it's a sheep, I mean. There was streaks of red on its back, its mother's blood, but that didn't mean she was hurt. I knew that from last time.

The ewe breathed deeper. Her belly in and out. Her eyes went soft, but in a good way.

The lamb, it was something beautiful.

Its little eyes and mouth.

Ears and feet.

Still on its side.

I went in close.

'Don't touch it,' he said.

I already knew this. If you do, the mother might abandon it.

We watched the lamb, its shaky legs as it tried to stand. It called out to its mother. She turned to the lamb, then more came out of her bum. A red, slippery mess. I remember how, the first time I saw it, I wondered if it was another lamb, but gone wrong.

'Just the afterbirth,' he said.

I didn't know what the afterbirth was back then, but it looked pretty disgusting. Same this time. But this time, the mother sniffed it. Then, she started to eat it.

It made me feel a bit sick.

He gave my shoulder a squeeze. He smiled, gold tooth.

'It's just their instinct,' he said. 'So the foxes won't get the scent, so they don't come for the lambs. It's natural.'

Foxes.

He mentions them sometimes, but I've never seen one. He reckons people don't think there are any foxes here. But there are, he tells me. They kill the rabbits, lambs too. He's seen them a few times on the low parts of the hill, near the farm, but he usually scares them off with the rifle.

'We've been lucky so far,' he said. 'But now it's lambing time again, we'll need to keep an eye out. With the drought, they might come closer. There's less food around, so they might get desperate.'

That's what my father tells me.

•

There's no picture in the encyclopedia, but I'll draw one from how it's described. It's probably not exactly right.

And this is the lamb who came today.

It's even more beautiful in real life. Most things are like that. Beautiful things, I mean. You can't describe them properly just with words. Can't draw them either. You need to see them with your eyes.

eleven

A while since I wrote, but I've been busy.

In the last few days, three lambs were born, counting the first one. They are all really beautiful.

My father seems a bit happier too. Hard to be sure, but I think so. More like old times. Before the drought. Before the man with the deep voice came.

I go down each morning to watch the lambs. I asked when I can touch them, and he said to wait a little bit longer.

They sleep most of the time, or drink their mother's milk, but all three have bonded with their mothers. That's what he calls it, *bonding*.

It's another word with more than one meaning, but this is the right one.

bonding
process by which a mother becomes emotionally attached to
her child.

I wonder sometimes why words have to be so difficult, why they didn't just make a separate word for everything.

Would be easier. For me, anyway.

Two of the lambs were born to one mother, and the other (which was the first one, the one I drew a picture of) on its own.

The first one I named Daniel, which is the name of an actor I saw in the *Women's Weekly* magazine. His name is Daniel Day-Lewis, and he was in a movie called *In the Name of the Father*.

Movies used to be on something called a television, which everyone watched in town. Every house had one, and they controlled your thoughts. My father told me about them in a lesson.

television
system for reproducing on a screen visual images transmitted
by radio signals or cable.

He explained they were part of the lies people told themselves, part of what people thought they needed.

'Like your mother.'

That's what he said. But then his eyes went soft. So I didn't ask him anything else.

In the Name of the Father was a drama, but I don't know anything more about it.

drama

play for stage or broadcasting.

Daniel Day-Lewis has a nice smile and warm eyes, and I wonder if he's still alive somewhere, or if he died in the plague. The actor, I mean.

My father explained once that movies were make-believe, but I didn't really understand. It's what actors and actresses did before the plague, people like Elizabeth Taylor.

The other two lambs are *siblings*, which is the word for a brother or a sister, so I gave them names of real-life ones. Siblings, I mean. I learned what siblings meant in a lesson too, but we haven't been having as many lessons lately. I don't really miss the lessons so much, but I wouldn't say it to him.

Even though he seems happier since the lambs were born, my father hasn't been spending as much time with me. After breakfast, he always seems to rush off to do some work on the farm. At night, he's more quiet than normal, so we go to bed earlier.

One night I woke up and he was standing over my bed. He didn't say anything, and I pretended to be asleep. He was just standing there, breathing, and I kept pretending I was sleeping until he left.

It felt strange.

I called the lambs Patricia and Rosanna, which are the same names as two sisters in the *Women's Weekly* magazine. Their second name was Arquette, but I only give sheep first names. Only actors and actresses have two names like that.

Sometimes I get Patricia and Rosanna confused, because they look pretty much exactly the same, and have the same mother. Patricia seems to be the one who drinks the most milk, and Rosanna walks around looking lost. Rosanna is my favourite.

I can tell Daniel apart because he has his own mother and sticks beside her like glue.

'Bit of a loner, that one.'

That's what my father says.

The lambs don't play much with each other, or with me, but it's because they're still too young.

It's usually like that.

When they're older, it'll be better. Definitely.

twelve

He was back again last night.

They talked for longer this time, and it was different because the man with the deep voice did most of the talking. I couldn't tell exactly what he said, but he laughed a few times. They both did. They seemed to get along better than the last time.

But I heard one thing my father said, right at the end.

'I gave you my word.'

That's what he said.

Then they both laughed, but not at the same time.

It was hard to sleep after.

In the morning, he was gone. I thought about asking about him again, but I didn't know how my father would react. He might be angry with me for asking too many questions, and

I'd see the whites of his eyes. The last few days, he seems angry all the time.

I think he could see my thoughts anyway, could see right through my eyes.

So I decided not to say anything.

Not this time.

·

It almost rained after breakfast. The sky got really dark, and I could see even darker clouds over the hill, lightning too. But then the clouds went the wrong way.

He acts funny when it gets like that. He doesn't say much, but he's outside a lot doing things, keeping busy. It's like he doesn't want to look at the sky too often, in case him looking at it makes a difference. Or being near me.

But I looked at it, and I was disappointed, because I know he'll be disappointed. It means he might get the soft eyes, even though we've got the lambs now. He might get the soft eyes and then stay in bed.

I hope not.

·

He waited til after dinner.

He'd gotten another rabbit and tried to roast this one. It was tough and pretty disgusting. We had some potatoes, which were okay. They're the only thing still growing, and only sometimes.

He leaned back in his chair, crossed his arms.

'Which one then?' he said.

'What do you mean?'

I knew exactly what he meant.

'The lambs. You've been watching them pretty close, so which do you reckon?'

I shrugged.

'What about the wool?' I said. 'And the milk? Like for the porridge that time.'

I didn't have my list with me, but I remembered.

He leaned forward, opened the door to the pot-belly, threw in another piece of wood.

'We've still got the other sheep for that,' he said. 'And don't you think we deserve a treat? Can't just have rabbit all the time. Or goat.'

I wish he'd make the damper instead, like my mother used to, and like he did for my eighth birthday. But I didn't say anything. He took his plate and scraped the bones into the fire.

I looked at the last of my dinner. I didn't want any more.

The fire whooshed from the wind outside. The wind outside gets down the chimney sometimes, like it's looking for us, and I could tell he was still waiting for my answer.

'Soon,' I said.

I said it as quietly as I could.

'Soon what?'

'I'll decide soon, but not right now.'

He smiled. Gold tooth.

'Good boy.'

•

Sometimes he tells me things. Things from the past.

It's usually after dinner, by the fire.

Or sometimes in his room.

He tells me without me even asking.

He says it started before I was born.

It's what made us come from the commune. From the town before that.

My mother and him.

I came later.

plague
an epidemic disease that causes high mortality; pestilence.
any widespread affliction, calamity, or evil, especially one
regarded as a direct punishment by God.

I've looked it up before, but I wanted to check again. He's never really explained it like the dictionary, though.

'The others came after. They came after the plague spread and infected everyone. They came because they're survivors, like us. But they're different from us, because they're carriers.'

That's what he said.

'A carrier's someone who has the plague and gives it to other people, but doesn't get sick themselves.'

To be honest, this doesn't make a lot of sense, but I don't know why he'd make it up. It's the first time he's said that word.

Carrier is another word with different meanings, but I think this is the one he's talking about.

carrier

person or animal that may transmit disease etc. without
*   suffering from it.*

I'll try to draw a picture of a carrier. I'll do it with the lumps, because that's what he says is a sign of the plague. He checks me over sometimes, just to be safe.

Don't know for sure if the carriers have the lumps, but it's just a picture.

'It started slow,' he said. 'People were getting sick, but most thought it was just the flu. Once people started dying, there was panic.

'Some people wore masks and gloves, or locked themselves in their houses. Others acted like nothing was happening, and said everyone else was crazy.

'Some people looked for a cure, and some tried to get the government to do something.'

I asked him about the government, and he said it has to do with the politics and the lies in the town. I didn't really understand, but I didn't say so, because I didn't want him to get fired up about it.

'Some people thought it came from rats. But that was a different type of plague. One from the olden days. Other people got angry and marched in the streets. There was looting.'

Looting is where people smash into the shops and steal things. He explained this to me, so I didn't have to look it up.

'But everyone was pretty scared, even if they all acted differently.'

That's what he tells me.

'We went to the commune after that. Me and your mother. But after a while, the plague got there too. People got infected. They wouldn't admit it, but I could tell.

'And we still had the farm. We had the farm because I knew we'd need it one day.'

I don't remember any of this, because it was before I was born.

He says it's probably just as well.

But I do remember some things. I remember how last time he told me that people in town didn't see it coming. They didn't do anything to stop it. That's different than what he said this time.

The story changes sometimes, just a little bit.

thirteen

Tonight I will write what happened in order, because that's how he said I should do it. It's how I should write things.

It's been a long time since I wrote here. I've been scared to. It's all been so different. But I have to start at the beginning.

Those are the rules.

I wanted to write about what happened, and what I found.

I had to check back to the first page, just to be sure. To see what the rules were.

Those are the rules.

•

My father went to town. He went after breakfast. After we had a lesson.

'Gotta get moving,' he said. 'Or I won't make it back by dark.'

He stood in the kitchen with the rifle slung over his shoulder. On the table, his plastic bottle, filled with water from the tank. The hessian sack too.

'Be careful,' I said.

He looked at me, smiled. Squeezed my shoulder.

'I'm always careful. And we need more oats, at least til it rains and things start growing properly again.'

He didn't mention the bullets, but I knew he was going for those too.

I watched him through the window. I watched him closely.

He climbed through the fence on the other side of the big dam. There's a small clearing after that, which leads to some scrub beside the hill. He doesn't go directly over the hill to get to town, but around it.

That's about all I know of how to get there, only that it's on the other side of the hill. And it's a long way off. The commune is even further, but I don't know where exactly, or even if it's in the same direction.

He goes to the shops in town, the ones that were looted. People's houses too. He goes through the dead people's things, the ones who died from the plague. Takes the oats and the bullets from their cupboards.

'They won't be needing them,' he says.

Even if it sounds a bit scary in town, I'll go with him one day. And if he doesn't take me, I'll go on my own.

•

I was pretty hungry at lunchtime, but there was only goat left, and it looked even more disgusting in the daylight. The skin and fat really sticks to the meat and gristle. It's hard to describe the smell, but it makes your lip curl up all by itself, without you even thinking about how disgusting it tastes.

I decided to wait for dinner. Hopefully, he'd bring back some oats. Maybe even something else.

A few times, he's brought back cans of baked beans. They're not really baked though, not like the rabbit or the goat are sometimes. They don't taste like smoke the way the rabbit and goat do.

The beans are in a sweet red sauce like nothing you've ever tasted. We usually have one can each, which he warms up on the fire. I asked him once why they were in steel cans, and he said it was so they would keep fresh a long time. Sometimes, if he's in a good mood, he gives me extra from his can.

Ever since we first had them, I always hope he'll bring back more of those.

·

I went outside and checked the pit. I knew there wouldn't be anything good, but I just wanted to see if there was much more goat. I was hoping there wouldn't be, that it was the last of it on the bench.

Me and him dug the pit. It took ages. The old one had caved in and was a bit further from the house. My father did that one when I was too young to help. When we dug the new one out, he put a barrel inside it, and got a wooden lid for it. It helps keep the meat fresher, but not forever.

'Keeps the animals away from it too,' he said, which is probably true.

Don't think many animals would be keen on the goat, though. Not even the foxes.

The lid is made of wood, but with hessian over the top. I lifted the lid and the smell was disgusting. A bit of the goat was still down there, but not much. It's just a knee or some kind of joint. I could hardly look at it, and I held my breath but could still taste it on my tongue. It had started to go all liquid, swimming in its own juice.

A crow let out a long, lonely call from down at the edge of the farm. The sun was in the sky over the top of the hill, and beyond the hill is the town. I figured he'd already be there. He's always back by dark, so it makes sense he'd get there by lunchtime.

And that's when I saw something.

Not just something.

Someone.

It wasn't him.

It was someone else.

And they were coming over the fence.

One of the others. The man with the deep voice. The man he was talking to.

I ran up the steps as fast as I could, and pulled the door shut behind me. I got the board and lifted it into the bracket, but I couldn't get it right in, not completely. I pushed it as hard as I could, like I'd seen him do, but it still wouldn't go down.

I ran to my room. I shut the door, pulled the sheet over the window.

I waited.

I waited, and it didn't take long.

Footsteps.

Heavy footsteps outside in the dry grass. Close to the house.

I should've got the big knife from the kitchen, but it was too late. I didn't want him to hear me. Didn't want him to know I was inside.

The steps.

Then, three knocks at the door.

Silence.

Three more.

I tried to slow my breathing. To make it go quiet. It didn't work.

'Hello?'

A voice from outside.

'Hello? Anyone home?'

Different from the deep voice. More gentle. Softer.

A woman?

'Hello? Is anyone home?'

Eventually, after forever, footsteps back down the steps.

•

I waited.

I waited for as long as I could.

I looked out the window.

I went slowly back out into the hallway, the kitchen.

And it was there.

Right there on the floor.

A sheet of paper, folded in half. Must've pushed it under the door.

I looked out the kitchen window, the paddock, and down to the fence.

No one.

I picked up the paper.

A note.

Must've read it a hundred times since.

Over and over.

Can remember what it says now, almost without looking at it.

I've read it, and read it again.

And this is what it says.

This is what it says, exactly.

I'm not even sure this is the right place, but I remember you saying you had a house up this way. There aren't many up here, so I just thought I'd say hello.

It's Chrissy. Hope you remember me.

Just came by to visit. Was sure I saw someone outside, but maybe I was imagining it. Hope you're both okay.

God, it's a million miles from anywhere!

I've left the commune now too – almost five years ago, actually. Jeff decided to stay, but Jessie came with me. She's 17 now – can you believe it?

I know when you left, we weren't on the best of terms. But things change, and time is the great healer.

Anyway, I hope you find this letter.

But if not, and maybe more than that, I hope you both found some peace.

x

Christine

PS – I'm up in these parts camping with Jessie. There's some beautiful walks. She's about to head back home, but I'll stay up for a little while longer. I'll come past again. Hopefully, if you're here, I'll catch you then.

fourteen

I haven't showed him. Not yet.

Don't know if I should. If I show him, he'll know.

He'll know I was outside.

He'll know she'll be back.

But if he finds it, and I haven't told him, he'll get angry. The whites of his eyes. And the bendy stick might come back.

So I've hidden it. The note, I mean.

I've hidden it in the back cover of my diary, so he won't know. So he won't see it by accident.

Gives me some time to think.

Some time to decide what to do.

·

When he came back, I had to pretend. Had to pretend nothing happened.

He didn't have any baked beans this time. Just bullets and oats.

I stayed quiet.

Christine.

Christine from the commune. And Jessie.

I wonder if Christine's one of the others. But it was daytime, so she couldn't be.

Maybe she's one of the ones he's mentioned, one of the ones with the plague, but who wouldn't admit it.

It's hard to know. But I can't ask him. Can't say anything.

She said she'll be back, but I don't know when.

I've still got time to think.

Time to work out what to do.

Writing about it might help.

It does that sometimes.

fifteen

Mushrooms are one of my favourite things. Picking them, I mean.

They grow up on the hill, mostly in autumn and winter. They're white and they live close to the ground, with dark fleshy bits underneath. You have to know which ones are good for eating though, because some are poison. The coloured ones, mostly.

That's what my father tells me.

poison
substance that when introduced into or absorbed by a living organism causes death or injury.

I like picking them, because we have a competition to see who can find the biggest one. It's a good competition, probably better than the running race, because I can win without him letting me. It's almost as good as yabbying.

We used to do that a bit, picking the mushrooms, but not so much lately. Mainly because it hasn't rained enough, so they haven't been growing.

We pick them on our walks. On our walks together, he talks about different things than the lessons, or the things on the farm. Bigger things.

'About life and the universe.'

That's what he tells me.

Last time, he talked about death, which he's never really talked about before. Not on our walks, anyway. We were up on the hill, on the trail, when he said it.

'There's no meaning in it. The only meaning is in living, in how we live while we're here. In what we do with our lives.'

He stopped and looked at me. He looked at me and through me all at once.

'Your mother never understood that,' he said. 'I thought she did, but she didn't. Everything was going to be different up here. But she couldn't see. I tried to make her see, but she couldn't.'

He touched my shoulder, then squeezed it. And I could tell that was all he was going to say about it.

We didn't plant them or anything. The mushrooms, I mean. They just grow wild, which makes them even better.

He does the cooking. He cooks them in the copper frypan, and they smell funny and shrink right down, but taste really delicious. They don't taste like anything else I've ever had before, and they fill you right up, even if they don't look like they will.

So that'll be one of the good things. One of the best things, really, when it starts raining again. Even better than the crop, I think. Maybe even better than the yabbies. Nearly as good.

Thought I'd write about it, because it takes my mind off the note and Christine and what I should do.

Haven't worked it out yet.

Maybe she won't come back. Maybe she won't come back and I can keep it a secret. He doesn't need to know. It'll just make him worry. Or get angry. Or get the soft eyes.

One of these things. None of them good.

It'll definitely be one of the good things when it starts raining again.

The mushrooms, I mean.

sixteen

Today he helped me water the crop, which was good because I really hate doing it on my own.

It's one of the worst jobs on the farm, definitely. Up there with the sewer and killing the mice.

You have to get water from the dam in a bucket, carry it up to the plants near the big dam, then to the crop. Takes ages, and he usually watches to make sure I'm doing it properly.

Two buckets for each plant.

The sun was out, and it felt warmer than it has been.

It was a long walk from the dam, so there was plenty of time to talk. Plenty of time for me to ask.

'What was it like?'

'What was what like?'

'When you and my mother first came here, from the commune.'

'Much the same.'

'Was the house here?'

'Yep. It was a bit nicer back then.'

'Nicer?'

'A woman's touch, you know. Things like decorating and baking, keeping the place looking good. Feminine things. She was good with that.'

'Did you miss it?'

'What?'

'The commune?'

He shook his head.

'Did my mother?'

He tipped the last of the dirty water from the bucket over what used to be carrots, but now is just dirt. I could smell his sweat. A bit like mine, but stronger.

'Sometimes. But there was no choice, not once the plague started infecting them.'

'What about the other commune people?'

'What about them?'

'Were any of them good? I mean, were they all bad? Were they all infected?'

He looked at me, but didn't answer.

'Did you ever go back?'

'No.'

'Did anyone come looking for you?'

He eyed me.

'Like who?'

'Well, didn't people from the commune wonder where you'd gone? Or what happened?'

He put the bucket down. His look scared me a bit, but I tried not to show it.

'What's with these fucking questions all of a sudden?'

'Just wondering, that's all.'

He stared. I could tell he was trying to look through my eyes again, to read my thoughts. I tried to hide them.

It felt like ages before he said anything.

'Some people came once. Do-gooders. When your mother was still here.'

'Who were they?'

'It's not important. They won't be back.'

'What happened to them?'

He crouched down, pulled a weed out from the dirt. Some plants are weeds because they can't be eaten. Some can be poisonous too, like the mushrooms.

He smiled. Gold tooth.

'Don't really know.'

'Did you let them in?'

He threw the weed into the dry grass. It was bright green against the yellow. Healthy looking.

'They might've had the plague. Couldn't take the risk.' He passed me the bucket. 'I'll go get another one, you head down to the dam.'

•

I was happier than usual to go to the dam. The sheep were there, and so were the lambs. I can touch them now, and they're beautiful. Daniel is my favourite at the moment, probably because he's mostly on his own. And he always looks at me when I'm coming, like he knows he's my favourite.

I haven't thought about which one. He hasn't asked again, so I'm not saying anything. And I've had other things to worry about.

do-gooder
well-meaning but unrealistic or patronising philanthropist or reformer.

I don't really understand what that means, not exactly. But I wonder if they ended up joining the others. Maybe as revenge for him not letting them in.

I wonder if Christine is one of the do-gooders. Jessie too.

The dam is pretty empty. The banks are looking deeper, and the mud is dry and cracked.

He came to the dam with a bigger bucket. The sheep ran off when he got close. He took off his boots, his socks. Rolled up his pants. He stepped a little way into the water, scooped up as much as he could, then held his hand out for my bucket.

'What happened then?' I said.

'When?'

'After the people were gone? The do-gooders.'

He laid the bucket almost flat, but only a bit got in.

'Nothing happened.'

'What about with my mother,' I said. 'What happened to her?'

He passed back my bucket, half-full.

'You know what happened.'

It's true, I do know what happened. Little bits of it. The bits he's told me. And the crying.

But I don't know what happened *exactly*. Exactly what killed her. That's what I was asking.

'Why did she die?'

He stopped filling the big bucket.

He looked at me, and I looked away. But I could feel his eyes. I could feel the eyes of the sheep too from across the paddock. They were all wondering why I asked, why it matters now.

But it does matter, I think. It matters how it happened. That's why I asked.

His voice came out low, from deep in his throat.

'Your mother was sick, very sick. In her mind. And she wouldn't listen to me. So she died a bad death.'

He passed me his bucket.

A bad death.

He's never said that before.

He stepped out of the water, picked up his bucket, but didn't look at me.

It was all he was going to say about it, I could tell.

•

When you ask something matters almost as much as what you're asking.

Sometimes, anyway.

I thought most deaths were bad. So I wonder what made hers especially bad, but I can't ask him.

Not yet.

But it makes me think that if there's a bad death, there's probably a good one too.

death

irreversible ending of life; fact or process of dying or being killed.

The dictionary doesn't say anything about good deaths or bad deaths, and neither does the encyclopedia.

So I'm just guessing what one would look like, compared to the other. I can't be sure.

This is a good death. It's probably like sleep, I think.

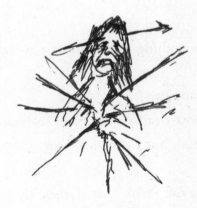

That's a bad death.

seventeen

Something happened. Something terrible.

This morning, or maybe last night.

The other sheep were on the far side of the paddock. They'd all turned away, facing the hill.

Maybe they saw the whole thing, but were pretending it never happened. Maybe they felt guilty for not stopping it, for letting it go on.

But there wasn't much they could have done.

·

His throat was torn and belly ripped open.

Tubes and organs, red and purple.

The fat green blowflies.

If I'm honest, I nearly cried. I nearly cried, because it's one of the lambs.

Daniel.

I couldn't really be sure at first. Eyes black and shining, open to the sun.

'She must've left some,' he said. 'The mother. She must've left some of the afterbirth.'

He said it more to himself, I think, than me.

His eyes went soft. Like he was looking at something hidden, or something from before. It's hard to explain, but it isn't good.

Isn't good for him, or me.

I wondered if it was because Daniel was dead, or because he didn't get to cook him. I think it's the first one.

'Go get the sack,' he said.

'What for?'

He saw what I was thinking, saw it in my eyes.

'For fuck's sake, we're not gonna eat him. Apart from anything, he'd make us sick.'

'Sick?'

'From the fox. They're full of disease.'

The fox.

I looked down again at the blood and guts, his little head and ears. I'd stopped any tears coming, swallowed them down.

'We'll need to clean it up,' he said. 'So more don't come.'

He made me do it. I'm not sure why, but I think he was trying to teach me something. That's usually why he makes me do something terrible.

He'll usually explain after, that it's to teach me something. Or sometimes, to teach me a lesson. *Teaching me a lesson* is different from *teaching me something*.

Daniel's head is the first part I put in, and I do it gently. One of the sheep starts calling from across the paddock, and I wonder if it's his mother. He goes and shoos them away toward the fence, nearer the hill.

I'm less gentle with the other bits, but still careful. Especially with his feet, which are so small. I'd gotten most of it in, but there was still other bits caught in the grass. Streaks of blood on my hands.

He came back, watched me.

Tears rolled down my cheeks, but I kept the sound in, hoped he didn't see. You can do that sometimes. I've learned how. You just need to hold it inside your belly, try to think of something else, and it eventually goes away.

This time, I thought of a picture in the *Women's Weekly* magazine. It's a picture of a yellow car with a lady driving it, though it doesn't say who she is. She's smiling and has red lips like Elizabeth Taylor, like my mother, but I think the picture is mostly about the car.

I've never seen a car before, not in real life, but he's explained them before in a lesson.

Daniel Day-Lewis.

I thought about him, the one in the magazine, with his nice smile and eyes. Tried to imagine what he'd do, if he was here. What he might say to us, to make us feel better.

'Where will we put him?' I said.

My father sighed.

'Away from here. Up the hill.'

•

He walked ahead of me in silence. When we got to the fence, he pulled up the wire so I could get through more easily with the sack.

We walked up the trail, blood dripping down the back of my legs.

'Won't he come?' I said.

'Who?'

'The fox. Won't he come for the rest of it?'

He shrugged.

'It's away from the farm, that's the main thing. And if they come up here, they might look for goats instead.'

They.

That's what he said. I wonder if he thinks it might not have been the foxes, but I don't say it. I know when not to say anything, not to ask.

Mostly.

We walked past the trail to where my mother is, then up the hill to where we collect wood, then further to where the trees close in and light from the sky almost disappears. A wattlebird called from the trees, and another answered further off, and I wondered if it was about us. I wondered if it was about us and what we had in the bag.

I know about wattlebirds, because he told me about them on a walk. He said they call out to their friends, and their friends call back. A lot of birds do this, mostly so they don't feel lonely.

That's what my father told me.

I thought about Christine and Jessie. Whether they were up there too. Whether they were on their way back from camping. Or maybe Jessie had gone home, like it said in the note. Maybe it was just Christine.

He pointed to where the land sloped away, where the trees are lower, angrier.

'There,' he said. 'In the creek.'

I've been to the creek before, but it's been dry for a while now. I could see where the water used to run, how the stones at the bottom are round and smooth, the soil a deeper red.

'Put him down there, in the bed.'

Bed.

Another word with more than one meaning.

I stepped down into it, the bed, with the bag over my shoulder.

I waited for a bit. Breathed in and out. I could hear him, back at the trail, gathering firewood. I crouched down and reached inside the bag, pulled out what was left of Daniel, piece by piece. Smeared in his own blood.

Tears caught in my throat, stayed there. I made them go back down.

I should have said something, but I didn't know what. And I wasn't sure it would have made things any better.

On the way home, I looked to the sky and it was a deeper blue, like the night was on its way.

Whatever else might come.

•

I got the fire going in the pot-belly. The wood was dry and it crackled and sparked.

He came in close. His face lit up orange, shadows beneath his eyes.

I closed the door to the pot-belly. I decided to ask him. It was the right time.

'What should I have said?'

'When?'

'When we left Daniel. Is there anything to say when that happens? When someone dies?'

He shrugged.

'People say things in a funeral sometimes, which is when they bury someone.'

I looked this up after.

funeral

the ceremonies for a dead person prior to burial or cremation.

'But we didn't bury Daniel,' I said.

He smiled. No gold tooth.

'He's just a lamb.'

Even if he was just a lamb, I would have liked to have said something. Something to show we cared about him. Maybe something about his life, even if it was short.

I wondered if his family, the sheep, might have done something. Done something like a funeral. Or if they just got on with things.

Maybe I'll go back when I get a chance. Go back and do it properly. But I won't tell him.

'What about my mother?'

He eyed me.

'Did we do a funeral for her?'

'Yeah, but not like a normal one.'

'What's a normal one?'

He shifted from the fire, sat back in his chair.

'A normal one has a priest, and starts in a church. And there are things that are said which are always said, but really make no difference.'

'Why didn't she have a normal one?'

He crossed his arms. Stared into the fire. Then into me.

'There's no church here, and no priest I'd ever welcome. So I buried her.'

The fire flared up. He leaned forward and opened his hands to the heat. His eyes went a bit soft, but not completely. Like he was looking a bit inside himself, for the memory.

'Did you say anything? When you buried her?'

His gaze went off somewhere into the distance, or maybe to the past with him and her. Couldn't tell which.

'Can't remember exactly. Maybe I did. Maybe I said some things we never said. Things I wish we had said. When she was alive.

'That's what happens at funerals. You say all the things it's too late to say. Some of them, anyway.'

He crossed his arms again. I could tell it's all he wanted to say about it.

It annoys me sometimes how he does that, how he just stops things before you can ask anything else. Before you can get to the truth.

He got up to get some goat from the pit, which was pretty much the last thing I felt like.

I tried to make my ears listen for the outside, to hear any noises. To hear if the sheep were calling out. To make sure the fox didn't come.

I can picture the lambs in my mind now. The bigger sheep are gathered around them in a circle, protecting them. What I'm imagining.

We could have brought them inside, but I don't think he'd agree. If it was just me here, I would for sure. Definitely.

Part of me still wonders. I wonder if it was the fox, or if it might have been the others. Maybe Christine and Jessie. Maybe he just doesn't want to say.

But I need to change something from before, because it's clearer to me now.

This is a bad death.

eighteen

They were talking again.
Last night.
It kept me awake.
Him and the man with the deep voice.
They were both laughing, like last time.
For a while.
Then, they argued.
I couldn't hear what they were saying at first, because of the wind outside. But I wanted to hear. I wanted to go up to his door and listen.
But I was too scared.
Too scared of the voices.
Too scared they might hear.

But then, the wind died down. And I heard my father more clearly. I heard him say something to the man with the deep voice. It was the last thing I heard him say.

'Can't make any promises.'

That's what my father said.

nineteen

It's been a while since I wrote, but I've been too tired.
Tired because of the talking in his room. Tired because
we've been going out every day.

Plus, the lessons are back on regular now. My father says I
need to be ready, so he needs to teach me as much as he can.

'While there's still time.'

That's what he tells me.

I wonder if it's about the man with the deep voice. About
giving him his word, his promises. But I don't ask.

We go out at dusk, because he says it's when they come out.
We go once, then a second time. A third.

The fox, or whatever it is, hasn't been back.

I've been looking every morning, checking on Patricia and
Rosanna and the rest of them. Something about them makes

me think they know. It's like they can feel they're in trouble. They move more quickly, closer together.

'Safety in numbers,' he says.

I'm not sure that's really true. It seems to me they're a bigger target, that they wouldn't be able to hide. I've always thought that's what I'd do, if the others came. I'd hide somewhere. There aren't many places to hide on the farm, but there's an old empty water tank. If I hide inside the tank, they won't see me. At least not straight away.

At dusk, when we go out, he crouches down for a long time behind a steel drum, the rifle leaning at his side. I'm beside him too, quiet like he tells me. He looks around the side of the drum, out to where the sheep are. The sky above the hill is red and yellow, like the fire in the pot-belly.

I haven't seen the smoke snake again. And there's been no sign of Christine. Or Jessie. I don't think they're coming back, but I can't be sure.

I look around the other side of the drum, but all I see are the sheep – no foxes. I see their fire eyes in the yellow light. They're worried about another night out in the paddock.

'Maybe the fox has got us figured,' he said. 'She knows our routine. That we go inside once it's dark.'

She.

I never thought of the fox being a girl, but maybe she is. It seems like a male fox would do more damage, but I'm not sure why.

'Maybe we confused her,' I said.

He looked at me funny.

'What do you mean, confused?'

'In the creek. The bed. With Daniel.'

Just writing his name now stings my belly. I can see his face again. His eyes, his ears, the blood. Hard to remember how he was before.

'Maybe they're going for the goats instead,' I said.

I'm not sure this is true, and I don't think he believes it. Lamb tastes better than goat. The foxes would know this, I think.

'It's the drought,' he said. 'They're coming closer, looking for food like I said.'

He looked up at the sky.

'If it doesn't rain soon, things are going to get tough.'

twenty

Something important happened. This morning, in the kitchen.
I'd made us the porridge. The porridge had dark spots
again, the droppings. My father hasn't asked me to kill the mice
anymore, and I can hear them in my room at night, running
around in the dark.

I tried to pick the droppings out of my bowl.

'It won't kill you,' he said. 'And I'll have to go to town soon
anyway. Get some more.'

'When?'

'Soon.'

'Can I come?'

He thought about it, scratched his beard.

'Not sure it's safe. Maybe when you're a bit older.'

He's been saying that for a long time now.

'I need to get some more bullets too, just in case.'

I wish he'd let me go too. But I figure when he does go, it'll give me time. Time for the things I want to do. Things which are harder to do while he's around.

Then, there was a noise on the roof.

We both looked up.

A few taps on the iron.

Then more.

He looked at me.

It came harder, faster.

'Rain,' he said.

He said it softly, almost like a question.

It came pouring on the roof like I've never heard before.

He stood up, rushed across the kitchen, and looked out through the window.

He smiled. Gold tooth.

First time in ages.

part two

part two

one

This morning, the rain was still falling. The sound on the roof was so nice, it made me want to stay in bed for longer. But my father had things for us to do.

We walked across the paddock toward the big dam. The ground felt softer under my feet, the grass smelled different. I looked across to the sheep – it was hard to count, but I could see both Rosanna and Patricia. I felt warm inside, in my belly. They were running around, chasing each other. They must like the rain. I wished I was there, playing with them. Wished Daniel was there too.

Maybe the fox has gone, was just passing through. And it probably wasn't the others. And Christine has definitely gone home. The do-gooder. Jessie too.

Things I tell myself.

You can do that sometimes, even make yourself believe it.

We stopped at the edge of the big dam, the reservoir, just where the bank starts to slope more steeply. He checked on his plants – they haven't been eaten for a while, but both the traps were empty.

'The rain will do them good,' he said.

But I saw something in his face, like the plants were good news and bad news all at once. I knew what he was thinking, but didn't say it. I can write it here, though.

If the rabbits aren't getting to the plants, or the traps, something is getting to them first.

I moved closer to the edge and looked down inside the dam. The reservoir. I can probably call it that again. Thick streams flowed down its steep banks, muddy water pooling at the bottom.

It isn't full though, nowhere near. Still, he smiled.

'All part of the plan. Get us fully independent again. Sustainable.'

Both words I've looked up before, but looking them up didn't help much. Still, I already know the plan, more or less. We need water to grow our own food, so he doesn't have to go into town anymore. The sheep are part of the plan too, but they don't know it.

He came close beside me. We looked down to the muddy puddle at the bottom.

'Could start you swimming again.'

'Really?'

'Might even get some fish.'

He smiled. Gold tooth.

He wanted to go down there. He wanted to see the water up close, to feel it on his skin.

He led me slowly down the stony bank. It was slippery, and his eyes told me to be careful. Somehow, it felt cooler down there, even though we were out of the wind. I couldn't see the sheep anymore, or the house. It was like we were somewhere completely new, somewhere away from the farm and everything.

We were halfway down when I saw it – on the far side, hidden away, where it's much too steep to walk. I wasn't sure what it was at first, but now I know.

It was a hole, a burrow. But not a rabbit's burrow.

It was much too big for that.

two

I've decided I might make a different rabbit trap, one that isn't so cruel.

I figure a good trap might be something which gets them inside a box, or a cage. But you'd have to trick them to go in first, maybe with something to eat. Then there could be a door which closes behind them.

Something like this.

I looked it up in the dictionary, but couldn't find anything I didn't already know.

trap

enclosure or device, often baited, for catching animals, usu. by affording a way in but not a way out.

Would be tricky for it to work, because you'd have to make it so the door would close behind it, and close hard enough that the rabbit couldn't get back out. You could probably fix that by watching the trap, and maybe pulling a string or something once the rabbit went in. But you couldn't watch it all the time.

The other thing I haven't worked out is what you'd do after. I mean, you'd still have to kill the rabbit. You could shoot it, but then there's probably no point to having the trap.

I'd probably drown the rabbit in the dam, just hold the trap underwater. I'm not sure if rabbits can swim, but I doubt it. It seems like a less cruel way to do it than snapping its neck in your hands. That's how my father does it.

He has three traps.

I don't like them, even if they protect the plants and give us rabbits to eat. They're all steel and vicious, with rusty teeth. They're too cruel, and there should be a better way. Like the trap I came up with.

I try not to think about how it happens. The snap of steel, the pain when they try to get loose. I wonder what they think about, caught there. I wonder if they think about their family, their father and mother. Or maybe what's to come.

I wonder what they imagine when they see him coming, his eyes like shiny black stones.

But I try not to think of these things.

He put one next to the plants, next to the one that's been eaten the most, as though it needs the most protection. I think the healthy one needs it more, but I don't say anything. The rabbits, if they're still around, would be more likely to eat that one.

But I think he has other things on his mind.

He went down the steep bank, closer to the burrow, and I followed behind. There was no sign of anything around the burrow, but I'm not sure what I was expecting. I didn't even know foxes lived in burrows, if I'm honest. I suppose I never thought about it much til now, but I thought they might just sleep in the bush under trees, or in the long grass.

The burrow looked deep and very black, and I wonder how far down it goes. I wonder if they were sitting there, listening. Or even watching us from the darkness. Maybe they're asleep, or maybe they're digging – trying to connect their burrows with the rabbit burrows. Maybe that's how they're getting the rabbits, and it's why we have to keep eating the goat.

He stepped on the spring of the trap and gave it his full weight. The jaws creaked open, and there's the little plate – the bridge – he shifted into place with his fingertips.

He took his hand away slowly, careful not to touch it. He remembers the two fingers back on the mantel, remembers to be careful.

The trap did what it's supposed to do, its jaws wide open.

'Wait here,' he said.

He went up the bank, reached into the grass. He came back with a stick, a dry twisted branch of a gum tree.

He handed it to me.

'What for?'

'Press the bridge.'

'What?'

He pointed to the trap.

'Why?'

'I want to show you something.'

Even with the stick, which was longer than my arm, I felt nervous.

'Go on,' he said.

I held the stick as close to the end as I could. I dangled it above the trap, then lowered it slowly. Closed my eyes.

The snap made me jump, crunched the stick in two.

'See? Now you know to be careful.'

But I already knew to be careful. I know from the fingers on the mantel. And I've seen enough rabbits to know what the traps can do. But this is him *teaching me something*. Like I said, it's different from him *teaching me a lesson*.

He re-set the trap, moved it to the side of the burrow, then covered it with dry grass.

'Otherwise, it's too suspicious,' he said. 'Animals prefer the shadows, places you wouldn't expect. They don't like being out in the open. Only predators like being out in the open.'

'But isn't the fox a predator? I mean, they hunt rabbits.'

'Yep, but they're hunted too.'

'By what?'

'Here,' he handed me the last trap. 'Your turn.'

I felt the weight of it in my hands. There was small bits of rabbit fur still left in its teeth, soft and grey.

I placed it on the other side of the burrow, where he showed me, tried to push it down with my weight. The steel bit into my feet. My boots are softer than his, almost worn through the bottoms. I pushed hard, but the jaws wouldn't budge. I tried to balance on it with both feet, using all my weight. Still, the jaws didn't move.

'You're not heavy enough. I'll do it.'

I stepped back. He placed one heavy boot on the spring, and the jaws released.

'You can do the bridge.'

This is the worst bit. The most dangerous. Somehow, it felt even more dangerous with him holding open the jaws like that. Like he could take his foot off and crush my hand, cut my fingers off to match his.

That would be *teaching me a lesson*. The lesson would be something like how I should never trust anyone, not even him.

I moved the bridge carefully, latching it into place. Part of me wanted to touch the bridge myself. Part of me wanted to see what happened when the jaws snapped on my hand, my fingers.

The feeling, it frightened me.

I took my hand away slowly. He lifted his foot, the jaws stayed open.

'Well done.' He smiled. Gold tooth.

'You have to learn these things. One day, you'll have to do it all yourself. When I'm not around.'

When I'm not around.

It's not the first time he's said that. More so lately.

I pulled some dry grass up to cover the trap as best I could. To be honest, I don't think the fox will fall for it. From what he's said about foxes, they're pretty smart. Smarter than sheep, and smarter than rabbits.

When they see something like this, just outside their burrow, they'll be pretty unlikely to step on it. I think traps have to be hidden properly, especially if you're trying to catch something smart.

The grass won't be enough, that's what I think.

three

Things didn't go like I planned. But it could have been worse. Much worse.

I knew I had to be quick, because I couldn't be sure exactly how long he'd be. It'd been a while since my father had gone to town, but he said he wouldn't be long.

'It's too risky now. I'll have to get in and out pretty quick.'

Not sure why it's more risky, but it wasn't the time to ask.

After he left, I waited. I waited for as long as I could. Long enough that I was sure he wouldn't turn back.

That's what I told myself.

•

There wasn't much left. His eyes were gone, the flesh of his face down to the bone. One ear was missing, the other half-eaten.

I think the crows had had a feed, but so had others. Rivers of black ants marched on a mission, all over his belly. His insides looked all shrivelled and dry.

My throat hurt, but I kept the tears in my belly. I thought about Patricia and Rosanna, and I hoped nothing like that happens to them.

I went down the bank, closer. I couldn't smell him as much, but maybe I was just used to it. The ants didn't seem to notice me, or didn't care, going on with their work. His ribs were exposed, his mouth open. There was no tongue, just tiny teeth coming through the gums. The ants rushed in and out of the holes of his eyes, keen for what was inside.

Soon, there wouldn't be much left. Just bones. Maybe not even that.

Daniel.

I reached into my pocket. I'd copied it down as carefully as I could. I could pronounce nearly all the words. Except the ones with the esses.

Our Father
Who art in heaven
Hallowed be thy name
Thy kingdom come, thy will be done
On earth as it is in heaven
Give us this day our daily bread, and forgive us our
trespasses
As we forgive those who trespass against us

And lead us not into temptation
But deliver us from evil
Amen.

I don't really know what any of it means. Except for the bit about forgiveness. And about evil. Both of those things, but not in the same way as this.

It wasn't in the encyclopedia, not under *funeral*, but it mentioned it. Said there's usually *prayers* at a funeral, so I looked it up in the dictionary.

prayer
request or thanksgiving to God or an object of worship.

It wasn't much help, so I tried the encyclopedia under P. It's called *The Lord's Prayer*. It's there as an example, I think. There must be others, but maybe it's the best one.

After I finished, I looked at Daniel and it didn't seem like the prayer had made any difference. But maybe it takes a while. For something to happen, I mean.

Then, I heard it behind me.

Coming through the bushes.

Footsteps.

Rough breaths.

Christine.

'What the fuck are you doing here?'

My father stared at me. He had the hessian sack over his shoulder, scratches on his face, his arms.

His gaze fell to Daniel.

My face went hot. I opened my mouth, but nothing came.

'I thought I told you to stay in the house.'

'I know.'

'Well, tell me then. What the fuck are you doing here?'

I wiped my cheeks. I hadn't meant to cry, I'd tried to stop it.

He sighed, then placed the rifle at his feet. He looked back over his shoulder, like someone might be watching, then at me.

'Why don't you listen?'

He lowered his voice, made it come out through his teeth.

'I'm sorry,' I said.

He took a deep breath in and out, put the hessian sack down. He took the paper from my hands. Studied it for a second.

'Where'd you get this?'

'The encyclopedia.'

'Do you understand it?'

'Not really.'

He scratched his beard. Breathed deep in and out.

'Want to know what it's about?'

I nodded.

'Well, it's just about trying to be a good person in life. Like some of the things we've talked about on our walks.'

'Why's it for funerals then?'

My father shook his head. 'It isn't just for funerals. I think this one is about being nice to other people, mostly so you get into a place called Heaven.'

Heaven.

'Is Heaven a town?'

He smiled. Gold tooth.

'Heaven is a place some people say you go when you die.'

'Really?'

'Yeah, but it's make-believe.'

'Like vampires?'

He frowned.

'Sort of. Some people say it's real, but it's just so you'll do what they want you to. Understand?'

I didn't really.

'It makes some people feel better about things, like when someone's died. Like there's meaning to everything. But there's really no meaning, even if they say there is. Especially with death, like I told you. The only meaning is in how we live.'

He looked down at Daniel.

'Poor bugger.'

He folded up my prayer, slid it inside his pocket. He looked at me more softly.

'Promise me you won't do that again. You won't come up here on your own.'

'I promise.'

He put the sack back over his shoulder, his other arm around me. His smell was like the farm, like the trees. He felt good and warm. It made me remember when we last came up for mushrooms. We might do that again, now it's been raining more.

Maybe the rain has helped. It's helped him be less angry. Haven't seen the whites of his eyes as often.

'C'mon,' he said, 'it's getting dark. And I've got some things to show you. I'll cheer you up a bit.'

•

He did have some things to show me.

Back at the house, in the kitchen, he emptied his sack onto the table. There was three bags of oats. They were different this time. They're called *Home Brand*. Must be the shop they come from.

There was two cases of bullets, the yellow cardboard boxes worn and broken. I could only read the writing on one of them. *Winchester .22 Calibre*, it said. The calibre of bullet has to be right for the type of rifle, it's got to do with the size.

'If you get it wrong, could explode on you.'

It's one of those things he's told me before, that I need to know for when he isn't around.

He got cans too this time, but not baked beans.

They were in the bottom of the sack, and they clunked and rolled heavy on the table.

It was something called tuna.

'It's fish,' he said. Gold tooth. 'I don't think you've ever had fish before.'

Fish are what he wants to have in the reservoir. But I didn't know they came in a can.

I picked up one of the cans and held it to my ear. I thought I could hear it moving.

'This is just the meat,' he said. 'They put it inside the cans to keep it fresh.'

The can had a picture of a tiny woman on it. She looks a little bit like Elizabeth Taylor in the magazine. I wondered what she had to do with the fish. Maybe she's the one who catches them.

She has a tail, instead of legs, and her name is Sirena. I didn't know how to pronounce it, so I didn't say it out loud.

'We'll have some for dinner,' he said.

Even though I didn't know what the tuna would be like, I was happy. It meant we wouldn't be having the goat. Anything is better than the goat. And he seemed like he was in a good mood, even if he'd caught me up on the hill.

But I'll have to be more careful from now on.

'A tuna fish isn't what we'll have in the reservoir. They're much bigger. And you can only catch them out in the sea.'

The sea.

We've talked about that place before in a lesson. And I've read a little bit about it in the encyclopedia. Mostly about a place called *The Pacific Ocean*. It's the biggest one, I think, and it's full of water. You can't drink the water though, because it's salty. That's what my father told me.

'There's plenty of fish who live in the sea, all kinds. The water is deep. And if you have a boat and nets, you can catch them.'

fish

vertebrate cold-blooded animal with gills and fins living
wholly in water.

This is what the can looks like.

Sirena must have a boat. Maybe she's
the captain. Boats have captains who
are in charge of everything. And there
are things called *waves*, which is when
the water flows in big walls that crash down
on top of you. I read about that as well. The sea and the ocean
are pretty much the same thing.

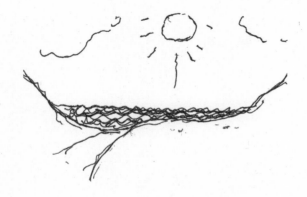

I wonder if my mother ever went there with him, if they
went there on a boat. I don't ask him, just in case he gets the
soft eyes and tries to look at all the things inside himself. The
things from the past.

Here's a picture. It's not exactly like the encyclopedia, because
I put hills and the sun in it.

'Will we go one day?' I said.

'Where?'

'To the sea?'

He smiled. It's the smile he does sometimes when he knows something I don't. Same as the smile when I ask things about the town. Or the commune. Or what happened before the plague. There's no gold tooth.

'Maybe,' he said.

But there are things I know about too. Things my father doesn't know. Like about Christine and Jessie and the note.

four

There's a sheet hung over my bedroom window, but it doesn't keep the sun out. It's blue and has pictures of dogs on it. The dogs are looking in mirrors. I don't really know why.

I've read a lot about dogs in the encyclopedia, and asked my father questions too. Dogs are like foxes or wolves. They once were wolves, but got domesticated, which meant they could live with people after that.

It was some sort of deal they did.

domesticate
tame (an animal) to live with humans.

He says we once had a dog, back when he and my mother were in the town, and at the commune. It was the same dog at both.

He was here on the farm too, but I don't remember him, I was too young. The dog's name was Dingo. Dingo is actually the name of a type of wild dog, which is like a wolf, but not exactly.

'Was supposed to be a joke,' he said.

I didn't really understand what he meant by that.

He says it was too hard to keep him, there wasn't enough food.

That's all he's ever really said about it. But maybe there's more to it. I'm not saying it isn't true, but maybe he's left bits out.

I don't know exactly what happened to Dingo. He probably left when there wasn't enough to eat. Maybe he's living somewhere else now, or maybe up on the hill. But I haven't seen him there.

Maybe he found another family to look after him, and he might come back one day.

That's what I think.

•

My belly makes a growling noise sometimes.

The tuna was salty and delicious, but there wasn't enough. I was really hungry when I woke up.

I went out to the kitchen, was careful to be quiet. The floorboards creaked, but I know the spots which are quieter. The pot-belly was still burning, red coals inside, and it was still warm in there. He must've put a log on before he went to bed.

I like it when he does that. It's like he's thinking of me.

I opened the door of the pot-belly and lit a candle from it, just for some extra light. The new oats looked good, no droppings in them, so the mice hadn't found them yet. I scooped some into the porridge pot.

And that's when I heard footsteps, crunching through the grass outside.

I froze.

But it wasn't Christine. Or Jessie. Or the man with the deep voice.

My father stopped in the doorway. He looked surprised to see me, even though I'm nearly always up before him. His eyes searched mine. It was like there was something smaller about him, something I *felt* more than I could see. Like part of him had been taken away.

It's hard to explain.

'Put your shoes on,' he said.

I didn't ask why. There are times when he says things and I know not to ask, or to answer. Not because of what he says, but how he's saying it. It's like the words close everything down at the end. Not the words exactly, but how they come out. This was one of those times.

•

I followed him across the paddock. The wind whipped down from up over the hill, where it was still dark. The sun rises at the opposite end of the sky, and it wasn't up yet, not completely. The whole world was still a deep, sour blue.

Their bellies were torn open, their guts spilled out on the ground. I didn't know which organs were which. I don't know a lot about that sort of thing, apart from with rabbits, but they're smaller. About the heart or the liver or the lungs. But I know they're all important.

Dark blood soaked the yellow grass. Patricia had her mouth open, like she was saying something when it happened, maybe calling out to the other sheep. To her mother. Or to me.

The other sheep had left them. They were off near the fence, looking at us. I wondered if they were expecting us to do something. Something to make what happened better. To take it all back.

I wondered if they watched. If they were sad, or scared, or both those things. Or maybe just happy it wasn't them.

Rosanna's head had almost come off, just some nerves and skin holding it there. Her eyes were gone.

'The crows,' my father said, seeing my thoughts. 'They took the eyes, not the foxes.'

I wonder why it is, why the crows like the eyes so much. Maybe because they're soft and moist. Or because the crows are just awful, evil birds. Both these things.

I hope it all happened quick. More than that, I hope they were already dead. When the crows came, I mean.

'I forgot the sack,' he said. 'You go get it.'

I was glad he sent me away. Glad isn't the right word, though. It was more like relief.

The tears didn't come as I walked back to the house, I'm not sure why. Not like with Daniel.

I got the sack from the kitchen, stained with Daniel's blood.

On the way back, I tried to think about Rosanna and Patricia when they were still alive. I tried to make myself upset, to prove I cared about them as much.

It didn't work.

five

L ast night, I didn't hear him talking.
I didn't hear the man with the deep voice either.
They weren't laughing, or arguing this time.
Neither of these things.
I haven't heard them talking at night.
Not since it started raining.
I did hear him though.
Wasn't sure at first, so I listened harder.
I listened for a long time.
Until I was sure.
Then, I listened and I waited until he stopped.
I couldn't sleep til then.
Not until he stopped.

six

My father goes every day at sunrise. I watch from the house. From my room. Behind the sheet.

He walks slowly, carefully. He circles and makes sure they don't catch his scent, so they don't know he's coming.

It's clever.

The sheep know what he's up to, though. They watch, but don't make a sound. They must know he needs quiet for this, that he's on their side.

He crouches down in the long grass, watching and waiting. After a while, he raises the rifle to his shoulder, and I close my eyes and hold my breath, waiting for it. But it never comes.

Once the sun is all the way up, he goes and checks the traps.

Every day, so far, there's been nothing.

Afterwards, I make us breakfast. Our spoons clink on the bowls, and I try to be quieter. I try to pretend I haven't been watching, that I haven't been up every morning.

Three days now.

But today, when I was done, I asked.

'Are the sheep okay?'

His eyes stayed down.

'Yes.'

'Did you see any?'

'Any what?'

'Foxes?'

'No.'

'Maybe they're gone then.'

He looked at me. Finished the last of his porridge.

'Maybe.'

'Could have gone up to the hill now, where we left the lambs. Maybe they're onto the goats, like you thought.'

He shook his head.

'They've got a taste for it.'

'But the other sheep, they're so much bigger than Patricia, Rosanna or Daniel. Even Charlene and David. They'll be able to put up a fight, I think. The foxes will find it harder with them, won't they?'

He didn't answer.

•

I wonder if dogs are friends with foxes, or if they're enemies. Maybe if we still had Dingo, none of this would have happened. If we'd been able to keep him. If he was still here.

But you can't know the future. You can't know what's coming.

That's what my father tells me.

I never saw Dingo, but I'll try to draw a picture of him. It's hard to draw dogs, because the encyclopedia has lots of pictures, and they all look different. They're all different breeds, different types of dogs.

I'll try to draw Dingo as halfway between a dog and a real dingo.

I can't show him, to check if it's right. Not while his eyes are like that. Maybe not ever.

seven

I was in the kitchen when it happened.
   When my father came in the house.
When he came in and told me.
'Get in your room.'
The whites of his eyes.
'Why?'
He smacked his fist on the kitchen table.
'Just get in your fucking room.'
I ran out to the hallway.
I did what he said.

.

I heard the door open, footsteps down the steps.
   Fast.

I waited for a bit, pulled a small gap, looked out the window. Nothing. Just the sheep. They looked like they always look.

I waited.

I wondered why he'd sent me to my room. Why he was so angry. What he was doing out there.

Voices.

I heard voices.

His voice. Someone else's. Not the deep voice.

Christine.

Must've been.

I looked out, but they must've been around the other side of the house.

I could hear him talking, the edge in his voice. But it was windy, and I couldn't make out exactly what he was saying.

She sounded different than last time, but it must've been her. Or Jessie. Jessie was heading back home though. It said so in the note.

But not Christine. She came back.

Like she promised.

I wondered if he'd bring her inside. I wondered if she'd tell him, tell him she saw me. Tell him about the note.

I waited.

There was nothing I could do.

But wait.

•

I sat down on the floor, and I listened to the wind. I couldn't hear their voices anymore.

Was a long time I waited.

I don't know how long, not exactly. But the wind had died down, and I couldn't hear anything.

I looked out the window. The sheep had moved nearer the dam, the sun lower in the sky.

Eventually, there were footsteps up the steps.

The door opened.

Movement inside.

He'd let her in.

After a bit, my door creaked open.

My father had the rifle with him.

I tried to read his face, his eyes.

'Come out,' he said.

'What's happened?'

'A visitor.'

'Who?'

He shook his head.

'It doesn't matter. She's gone now.'

I got up off the floor, followed him out to the kitchen. Him and the rifle. He placed it on the table, sat down.

I wondered what she'd told him, what he knew about the note.

'What did she want?'

He smiled. Gold tooth.

'It's not important. She won't be back.'

I sat down.

'Was she one of the others?'

He shook his head.

'Just someone who made a mistake. A big mistake.'

He eyed me.

'Did you see anything?'

I wondered what he meant. I wasn't sure if he was talking about this time, or the last time. If he already knew she'd been before, and was trying to catch me out.

'No.'

'You sure?'

'Yep.'

'Not a thing?'

My chest went tight.

'No.'

Was hard to lie, but I kept the truth in, kept it hidden. I kept it inside, buried it deep.

He scratched his beard.

'Well, either way, we need to be more careful now. There could be more coming.'

He stared at me.

'Might have to get on the move at some point. Might not be safe to stay here.'

Silence. His eyes on mine.

'Are the sheep okay?'

He frowned. 'The sheep? Yeah. Why wouldn't they be?'

I shrugged.

I knew the sheep were okay, but I didn't know what else to say. I needed something to fill the quiet in the air between us, to stop him staring at me. To stop him reading my thoughts.

The note in my diary.

Christine.

Jessie.

I decided right then that I'd get rid of it.

The fire.

That's the place for it.

I haven't done it yet, but I will.

Definitely.

I can't risk him finding it.

Can't risk him knowing what I know.

•

I need to find a better hiding spot.

For this book. My diary.

Somewhere he'll never think to look.

I'll think of something.

I wonder if she'll be back again.

I doubt it.

eight

I woke this morning to heavy rain. I'd been having a dream about Sirena.

We were on the boat together, me and her, and she was beautiful and strong. She was catching the silver tuna with her hands, lifting them out of the water. She had long, smooth legs instead of a tail.

The boat was wooden and we rode the waves toward the edge of the ocean, the sea, toward the sky. The boat had a name, but I can't remember it now.

She was smiling at me. The silver tuna smiled too.

I climbed out of bed, went to the window. I shifted the sheet and saw the dark sky outside. Rain spotted the glass, and I couldn't see the sun yet. But I knew he'd be happier. He'd be happier with the rain, and he'd forget about Christine, and the soft eyes would be gone for good.

That's what I told myself.

More rain means more water in the big dam, the reservoir. And the crop might even grow again.

I looked for him out there, through the rain.

I thought maybe he'd slept in. Or maybe he'd just given up on the fox. It's been a while now since the sheep were killed.

Then, I saw him.

I saw him walking slowly, coming up from the big dam. The rifle slung across his shoulders, coat collar pulled up, his face low and arms crossed.

He was carrying something.

It was something small and dark.

It was hard to tell from here, through the rain. But he looked different than normal.

It was hard to tell exactly, but it looked like he was smiling.

•

Her fur is thick and lush, her eyes the deepest black I've ever seen. Same as in the burrow, because that's where she's from.

She's so small and delicate, I can't believe she's done something so awful, so horrible, to the sheep.

'Just a young one,' he said. 'Got caught in the trap.'

Her ears pricked, listening to everything. Trying to know what's about to happen.

My father held out her back leg and I saw the matted fur, an open wound where the teeth had got hold. Her tail swooshed all lazy, eyes sparkled.

I wondered if it was the trap I set. I hoped not.

I hoped it was his, but I didn't ask.

He sat at the kitchen table, holding her. She smelled like wet gum leaves. There was thunder somewhere in the distance, and the fox sat up sharp.

'Shhh,' he said.

He put her on the kitchen table, she eyed me suspicious.

'Come hold her.'

I did as he said, holding her sides, keeping her still. I felt her small, tight breaths going in and out. Her fur felt rougher than I'd imagined, not soft like the sheep wool. She kept her sore leg up off the table, small drops of blood. Her blood looked darker than normal blood, ours or the sheep's.

She was frightened, I could tell.

The big knife, right there on the bench.

I closed my eyes. I closed my eyes and pretended it wasn't going to happen like this. It's the best way with things sometimes. Awful things. Pretend they're not happening, then try to forget them.

I heard water running in the sink. I opened my eyes, and he was squeezing out a cloth.

I watched as my father came in close, then carefully cleaned her wound. The fox flinched, twisted her head back toward my hands. I kept hold.

'Shhh,' he said.

She twitched, squealed, struggled, then finally relaxed. Her body small and hard, like she'd move fast if I let her go.

He pulled a hanky from his pocket, wrapped the wound tight. He tied a knot, then another.

'There, all good.'

He looked at me, and I think he saw what I was thinking, but didn't say.

It was all pretty confusing.

'Wait here,' he said.

I kept hold of her, but not too firm.

He went out the door, and I could see the rain was heavier, but the sun was up properly. I tried to look her in the eyes, to see what she was thinking. She looked away.

He came back with a piece of goat from the pit. It stank even worse than normal. He sat beside me, pulled small pieces off between his fingers, fed her gently.

At first she sniffed it, unsure. Then snapped it from his fingers.

He smiled. Gold tooth.

'She's hungry. You try.'

I tore a piece and it felt nervy. I held it close to her, she sniffed, then chewed it up all eager.

My father leaned back in his chair, put his hands behind his head. The smile was all the way up to his eyes. First time in ages.

'You can look after her,' he said, 'until her leg is better.'

nine

She lives in the old steel birdcage.

I never even knew we'd ever had a bird til now, or that the cage was a birdcage. It's from back when my father and mother lived in the town.

They brought some things from the town, when they came here. After the commune. At the commune, they weren't allowed to have things like that.

That's what my father tells me.

'It's an aviary.' He opened the small door at its side. 'That's what it's called, if you want to be more accurate about it.'

'What's an aviary?'

'Just a fancy name for a big birdcage.'

To be honest, I'm not sure why anyone would want to keep a bird. They wouldn't be much company. And they'd definitely be happier flying around.

On our walks up the hill, he likes to tell me about the birds who live up there. About the grey shrike-thrushes, wattlebirds, and the currawongs. Those ones, mainly. The currawong is like a crow, but much nicer.

He knows all about birds. About their nests and their calls to each other, and which trees are their favourites.

There's lots of birds up on the hill, but mostly just crows and magpies on the farm. I'm not sure why.

'Did we have many birds?' I said.

'Just one at first. A cockatoo named Joe. He could talk and everything.'

'Really?'

'Yeah. Well, he'd just copy what you said.'

It doesn't sound like it could be true. I can't imagine crows can talk, or magpies, or currawongs. He would have told me if they could. But maybe cockatoos are special.

He crouched down, put the fox in the bottom of the cage.

'Then we got a rosella. To give Joe some company.'

'A rosella?'

'They're smaller than a cockatoo. They're red and blue and green. Really pretty.'

'Could it talk?'

'Nah.'

He closed the door, slid the latch. The fox shot him a look.

'But Joe didn't like the rosella so much. So then it was just Joe again, on his own. Think he preferred it like that.'

The fox watched him, almost like she was listening to the story. He has this way of telling stories sometimes, where he doesn't tell you everything, and you have to figure out what happened.

In this one, it sounded like Joe the cockatoo killed the rosella, which is pretty awful.

'What happened to Joe?'

My father scratched his beard.

'We had to let him go.'

He didn't look at me when he said it. And I wonder if what happened to Joe was actually the same as what happened to Dingo.

'What about the visitor the other day?'

'What about her?'

'Do you think she'll come back?'

He shook his head. Smiled. Gold tooth.

'I doubt it. Actually, I'm pretty certain. She got the message, loud and clear.'

He headed back for the house, and left me with the fox. The fox licked at its bandage, which my father had made from his hanky.

I watched her, and she watched me.

•

I wonder about the lambs and whether she had anything to do with it. The fox, I mean. I wonder about Daniel's mum and whether she misses him. These two things, mainly.

I also wonder if he's right about Christine, but I'll just have to try not to think about that. Just try to forget it. It'll be easier that way. I've burnt the note now, so as long as he doesn't find this diary, he'll never know.

I wonder about the fox's parents too, her parents back in that dark, black burrow. Wonder if they know what's happened. If they might come looking. Maybe it's a trap, like my rabbit trap.

Maybe that's what he has in mind.

I looked up cockatoo in the encyclopedia, but there was nothing about whether they can talk. I checked the dictionary too, but it's not much help.

cockatoo
any of several parrots of Australia etc. having powerful beaks
and erectile crests.

I've seen them flying through the sky, but I've never seen one up close. So this is really just a guess.

It probably looks completely different.

ten

I found an old hessian sack today, under a sheet of tin. It was dusty as anything, but I gave it a good shake.

It's a potato sack, because there's a picture of a potato on it, and the name *Scottsdale*, which must be a type of potato. Must've been from a proper farm, before the plague and the others and all of that.

I opened the door and put the sack in the cage, next to her bowl of water.

She paced up and down, and each time she got to the end of the cage, she seemed surprised. I got a stick and poked it through the cage, to see what she'd do, but she ran to the other end and hit the steel mesh. I felt bad and threw the stick away.

She stared at me with those black eyes, licked at her bandaged leg. I'm not sure if she's happy or not.

My father called out from the house.

'Back soon.'

He headed off toward the reservoir. He probably went to check the water, seeing that it's been raining. Or maybe to re-set the trap, to try to catch her father and mother. If he does catch them, I don't think he'll be putting them in the cage.

Maybe we can train the fox, train her to be like Dingo. I'm not sure if my father will go for that. He got rid of Dingo because of food, so would probably do the same with the fox. Still, he could have killed her right away with the rifle or the knife.

It's hard to know. Hard to know what he's thinking. Even more than normal.

He said to look after her til her leg is better. But I can't think he'll let her go, not with the sheep and everything. Maybe we'll just keep her on a rope or something. Or the chain and the padlock and the key from his cupboard.

I said some of this out loud to the fox, but she just looked at me funny. I don't think animals can understand what we say, not really. It doesn't say anything about whether they can in the encyclopedia, or the dictionary, but I doubt it. If they could understand, they would have learned to say something by now. Except for the cockatoo.

When he was at the reservoir, I went to check on the sheep. When I got near, a few of them ran, which made the rest of them run too. That's the thing with sheep, when one does something, most of them follow. Usually all of them. It's probably not that clever, because they could be following a sheep who's a bit stupid, or doesn't think straight.

It's the first time they've ever run from me like that, and I wonder if they're nervous after what happened to the lambs. Or maybe they know we've got a little fox. Maybe they think we're going to feed them to her, or they can smell her on me – the wet gum leaves smell.

I checked the little dam, and it's looking pretty much the same. It's always hard to tell exactly, because it changes slow. When things change slow, they can change a lot without you realising it.

That's what my father tells me.

Still, I'll tell him it's looking more full, he'll be happy about that. Always better to stop the soft eyes before they start again.

A crow called from the fence next to the dam. There were two crows there, but only one was doing the talking.

'*Craaa*,' he said.

'*Craaa*,' I said back.

He flapped his wings a bit, like he was just airing them out.

'*Craaa*,' I said again, but he didn't answer me.

I picked up a stone from the edge of the dam and threw it at him, but missed by miles. It's not because I didn't like him or anything, but more about what happened to the lambs. He might have been the one who ate Daniel's eyes, or Patricia's, or Rosanna's.

But maybe not all crows like the same things, just like people. Like how he likes to eat the goat, but I don't. At least I think he likes the goat, but he's never really said so.

Still, maybe that crow was the eye-eater. He probably likes goat too, he looked like he might. I picked up another stone and threw it, but this one hit the fence post and gave both crows a fright. They took off into the air all black and horrible, and I tried to see where they were going, whether they were heading up the hill to where we left Patricia and Rosanna. I still haven't been there to give them a proper funeral.

I watched them fly, their feathers black and silvery blue, but I lost sight of both against the deep green of the hill. I wondered if Christine is still up there, or if she got the message like he said. I've been trying not to think about it too much, but it's hard.

Then, I saw it.

It was closer this time.

It's something I don't really want to tell him about. I don't want to tell him, because of the soft eyes. And because of the man with the deep voice. I don't want either of them to come back.

But I know I will have to tell him, that I should say what I saw. Probably soon. Because otherwise it could be a lot worse.

It could be like with Christine and Jessie, and I'll have to keep another secret.

eleven

My father doesn't talk about the years or the months very much. Not even the days and weeks. Mostly just the seasons. But he always tells me when it's my birthday, and that's when I know a year has gone past.

On my birthday there's no lesson, and we just have a walk. He even cooks the porridge in the morning, but he didn't last time. Last time, after he gave me this diary, we walked up the hill and he showed me the rings of a tree. It was a tree someone had cut down a long time ago, and you could see the rings on its insides. He told me that each ring is a year, like a birthday. We counted forty-three of them, which I thought was very old.

He smiled. Gold tooth.

He said some trees can live for hundreds of years, which might be true.

If it wasn't for my birthday, I wouldn't know when a year has gone by. But I can tell when a month goes past, more or less, because it's when we have the wash.

There's a shower in the house, over the top of the bathtub. We don't use it anymore, and I wish we did. It's connected to the water tank and he says it's a waste. It's been ages since we used it. More than a year, I think, but I can't be sure. When we used it, we still had soap. It made bubbles and stunk a bit. Been ages since we've had any of that.

We went down to the small dam. It was almost dark when we got there, and it was cold, so it really was the worst time.

'Better to get it out of the way now,' he said. 'Before dinner.'

We both stripped off at the edge of the dam, on the bank. My toes sunk into the slimy mud. That's the thing, the dam is muddy and not great for washing anyway.

When it's raining more often, we'll probably use the shower again. That's what I tell myself.

Before we went in, he checked me over, which is probably the worst bit. I have to stand in front of him, arms raised and legs apart, and he checks me for lumps.

'First sign of it.'

That's what my father tells me.

Have to check him over too, which is the second worst bit.

'Do it properly.'

If I see anything, I have to tell him. But I never see anything, and I don't like doing it. It's strange, but every time it's like I can't remember exactly what his body looked like the last time.

The way his ribs poke through his skin, and the dark hair on his chest.

'You'll be like this too one day,' he said.

'Really?'

'Well, not exactly like this. Just older. Different. All clear?'

'Yep.'

Sometimes, I wonder what would happen if it wasn't clear, if I found a lump. Would I tell him? I'd have to.

I wonder what he'd do. I mean, the plague is contagious. It spreads from one person to another. So if he caught it, I'd probably catch it too.

We'd have to live separately after that. Maybe he'd go away somewhere, maybe to the town, or become one of the others. I don't really like to think about it so much.

I think it's part of why he doesn't like to go to the town. The town is where the plague started, so he's worried he might catch it there. He's never said that exactly, but it's what I think.

We went down into the water and he passed me my cloth. It was so cold. I went up to my waist, soaked the cloth, and started washing. The sheep watched on all silent from near the fence. They must wonder why we do it, why we take off our clothes and go in the cold water they use for drinking.

Then, I said it.

'I saw something.'

He turned to me, squeezed his cloth in his hands.

'I saw something. Up on the hill.'

His face dropped a little, then went back to normal, like he made himself do it.

'What did you see?'

'Smoke.'

'Smoke?'

'Like, from a fire.'

He shook his head. 'You're imagining things again.'

I started to shiver. If you don't keep moving in the water, that's what happens. And if you stay too long, you start to shrivel up.

'Don't think so,' I said. 'I definitely saw it. About halfway up.'

He turned his back to me, started washing his hair with the cloth. His back looked hairier than I remember, and I wondered if the hair keeps growing when you get older.

'You'd be surprised,' he said. 'Your imagination plays tricks sometimes.'

This annoyed me a bit. I almost wanted to tell him about the note from Christine, just to teach him a lesson. To teach him a lesson for not believing me.

But I noticed something different in his voice. It wasn't like normal. It was kind of hollow, or emptier, if that makes sense. Like it came just from his throat, not down in his chest.

I crossed my arms to the cold, but it didn't help. The sheep bunched up closer together near the fence.

He turned back and his gaze met mine. I looked away. There was something different in his eyes, but not like the soft eyes.

I could see more of the white part. It made me nervous. Made me glad I didn't say about the note from Christine.

'C'mon,' he said. 'Hurry up, and we'll head back for dinner. I'll get the fire going.'

He splashed water at me, forced a smile. I could see the gold tooth, but I knew he was forcing it, because there was no reason to smile, not right then.

It disappeared really quick too.

•

Dinner was potatoes and porridge. The potatoes were green and hard, not cooked properly, but I still swallowed them down.

There was no goat left. I was happy about this.

'Have to head up the hill tomorrow,' he said. 'Do some hunting. Three mouths to feed now.'

The wind blew hard outside, and I could feel the cold come into the kitchen, up under my shirt.

'Will she be okay?' I said.

He eyed me. 'Who?'

'The fox. Outside. Now it's getting cold, I mean.'

He crossed his arms.

'They're used to being out in the weather,' he said. 'Have that nice thick coat. People even used to make clothes out of their coats.'

I imagine a coat made from a fox. Don't like the look of it.

'Your mother used to have a fur coat.'

I was on the last piece of the hard, green potato. It got caught in my throat, but I made it go down.

'Made from foxes?'

'Nah, something else. Mink, I think. A sort of rodent. Like a rat. Or a mouse.'

A coat made from mice sounds even worse, but I didn't say so.

'I got it for her birthday. You wouldn't remember.'

I don't remember, but I remember other things. I remember her in my room, his voice outside.

Sometimes, I'm not sure if I do remember, or if maybe I'm imagining it. Maybe it was a dream.

It's hard to be sure.

He hardly ever talks about her anymore. Not as much as he used to. He used to talk about her baking things in the fire. Things like the damper and the potatoes, and how the smell used to fill the house and make it feel like home. He'd nearly always get the gold tooth when he said it.

But when he talks about her now, it's different. He gets this funny look. It's like the soft eyes, but not exactly. It's like he's looking off into the distance somewhere, but not really. When he talks about her now, it's like he can still see her, but he's actually just looking at the wall, or the ceiling, or at me.

'Did she like it?'

'Yeah, it was real fancy. I got it from town. Would have cost a fair bit, if you paid for it. Your mother still liked those things. Material things. Things from the town.'

He was watching her on the wall, wearing that nice coat.

I tried to imagine her in a nicer-looking coat than one made from foxes, or the mouse one. Elizabeth Taylor with red lips and a nice warm coat. I wonder if she's wearing it now.

'She never wore it though,' he said.

'How come?'

He eyed me.

'She was hard to please, your mother. We didn't agree on things. A lot of things.'

'Like what?'

He scratched his beard.

'Sometimes, she didn't like it here so much. This life. And her sickness made things worse.'

He looked at me, through me.

'You'd never leave me, would you?'

I wondered if he was still talking to me, or to my mother in her coat. It was hard to tell, and I couldn't ask.

'No,' I said.

For a second, I thought he didn't hear me. But then he nodded and reached for my plate.

I could tell it was all he was going to say about it.

•

I wonder why my mother didn't like it here. And I wonder if he's still thinking about her now, in bed. Or maybe he's thinking about the smoke. I wonder if that's really why he's going up the hill tomorrow, not just for the goat.

He's looking for Christine.

I try to imagine the fire up the hill, with the others sitting around it. Might be some kind of trap, like he's doing with the foxes. They're trying to get us to go up there.

I've decided this is what they look like, more or less. I don't think they look like Larry Hagman anymore.

twelve

I ate breakfast alone, the sun only just up. I could hear my father getting ready, shifting things in his room.

He came out with the rifle in one hand, bullets in the other. Put both on the table.

'Hollow-point,' he said. 'The bullets. More powerful, these ones.'

He took one out of the box, held it up to the light, then passed it to me. All steel and brass, smooth and beautiful.

'The bit at the top is the bullet. The casing, the brass bit, is the gunpowder. That's what makes it go. In a rimfire, anyway.'

I already knew this, he's told me before.

'Rimfire.'

I say it out loud because I like the sound. The feel in my mouth. Some words are like that.

He took it from my fingers, put it back in the box, pushed the box into his pants pocket.

'Should knock them down with one shot now. More efficient. Will have to give you a go.'

'Really?'

'Yeah. Just a bit of practice first. Maybe when I get back. What do you think?'

His eyes shined, like he thought I'd be happy with that. So I made sure I looked like it.

'That'd be great.'

He smiled. Gold tooth.

•

She was sitting on the hessian sack. I was happy about this, because it makes me think she would have been warm last night, that she would have used it as a bed. Her water looked the same as it was, but I'm not sure how much foxes drink.

She hopped up when she saw me, shifted to the back of the cage. She went slow, carried her back leg.

'Shhh,' I said.

Her eyes sparkled, and her tail is the most beautiful thing – lush and dark like night.

She sat down, curled herself up.

'Do you miss your mother?'

Her ears shifted left and right.

'Will they come? Your father and mother?'

I poked my finger through the steel mesh. Her breaths went in and out, her belly up and down. She turned and licked her leg.

'Your brother? Sister?'

I went to the side of the cage, opened the door. She went further into the corner. I crouched down, reached inside. She was still tense, hard in my hands. I took her out, cradled her against my body.

Wet gum leaves, something else now.

I placed her on the grass. She moved slowly, turned to lick at her leg. I don't think she can run with her leg like that. Just as well.

'It'll get better.'

I stroked her gently along her back.

She sniffed the grass. I won't be able to teach her anything, not without the goat meat. I'm not looking forward to the goat for dinner. But at least, for once, it might be useful.

Could train her like the wolves got trained, like a dingo. She could be a friend for me and him.

It'll be better if there's three of us, instead of just two.

•

I knew it was a risk.

And I knew I wouldn't get off so easy this time, if he found me there again. But I'd been worrying for days. It didn't seem fair not to say anything for Rosanna and Patricia, seeing how I'd done it for Daniel.

If he found me, I figured I'd be able to explain. Maybe.

So I went earlier, not long after he was gone. I wanted to make sure he wouldn't come back before I could get to the house.

But I couldn't be sure.

•

I know the way now. And I was quick.

But there wasn't much left.

They must've eaten nearly all of it, the flies and the ants. Crows too.

Just a few bones in the creek bed. One of the skulls was there. I couldn't tell whose it was, but decided it must be Patricia, or Rosanna.

I started with the Our Father one, which Daniel had heard before, but not Patricia or Rosanna. I read it pretty quick. Then the new one, which is called *Hail Mary*. Found that one almost by accident. It was in the encyclopedia, in the M book.

It's about someone called *The Virgin Mary*. I looked up *virgin* in the dictionary, and it's someone who hasn't had sexual intercourse, which is what is used to make babies. But *The Virgin Mary* had a baby and its name was Jesus.

It all sounds a bit strange. I might ask him about it sometime.

I'm not sure if the *Hail Mary* is meant for funerals, it didn't say, but I figure it can't hurt. And it talks about the hour of our death, so it probably is.

He's probably right about there being no place called *Heaven*. But in case there is, it doesn't seem right that only Daniel would get in, and not Patricia or Rosanna. They haven't done anything wrong.

If I'm honest, I probably liked Daniel better, but that shouldn't decide something like that. It's too important. Especially now I know about the other place.

The other place is in the encyclopedia and the dictionary and it starts with H too. It's not a town either.

hell
place (of fire and other torment) regarded in some religions as the abode of the dead, or of devils and condemned sinners.

Anyway, I probably liked Daniel more just because I knew him better, because he was on his own.

When I was done, I put some branches over the top of the bones, like a burial. Then I said the Our Father one more time. I went back to the trail, down a little way, then took the path off to the other place, where my mother is. I went there because of what I know now, what I know about the two places you can go after you die.

It's probably too late for her, but still worth a try, especially if she's in the other place. Might help her change to the better one.

There was some flowers on the picket, looped into a ring. Small white flowers which grow on the hill sometimes. He must've visited her too. They were dry, so maybe it was a few days ago.

I found a nice branch with deep green leaves and poked it into the ground against the picket. It looked better like that, almost like a tree, but with a steel trunk and flowers. I squinted my eyes and it looked even more like it.

It's funny how things like that can make you feel a bit better. Like I remember once he put a wreath on her grave. A wreath is something you can make out of flowers and branches, and it was one of the most beautiful things I'd ever seen.

That was a long time ago now, and he only did it once. I think it was a lot of work. Making it, I mean. He stayed up working on it for three nights in a row, and he wouldn't tell me what it was for.

'It's a surprise,' he said.

And it was. For me and for her.

The branch I put there wasn't as nice as the wreath, but it still looked better than nothing. I said both prayers, and then said them again because it's been so long since she died. For it to work, you'd need extra.

When I was saying the prayers, I tried to picture her, her smiling face and red lips, and the nice warm coat on. But because she's down in the ground, it didn't really work. I didn't have enough time to imagine it properly.

•

Here's a picture of the other place. It's how I imagine it, anyway.

Sometimes, drawing things helps me stop thinking about them. Same as with writing.

If I put them on the page, they leave me alone.

Sometimes.

•

I tried not to watch as the sun went down behind the hill. As if by watching, it might go faster. But I could feel the air getting cooler, the wind getting stronger.

It was the latest he'd ever been, definitely.

I tried getting the fire going in the pot-belly. I gathered the small, dry twigs and bunched them together. It's important to keep space underneath for the dry leaves. I lit the leaves with a match, they flared and burned hot, but the twigs didn't catch.

I tried again, but there was no hope with the blackened twigs. Out the window the sky had gone dark, and there was a twisting in my belly.

The others.

Maybe the others got him. It was a trap, just like I thought.

I should've said something. I should've said something about it being a trap, because it could just be me left on my own. Just me and the sheep and the fox.

Even if he scares me sometimes, it'd be worse if he wasn't here. If I was here on my own, I mean. Just me and the fox. It'd be much worse. I can barely imagine it.

I went to the drawer in the kitchen and got the knife with the bone handle. It's the one I use for rabbits. He'd taken the big knife, because it's what he uses to cut up the goat.

But not this time.

This time, the big knife got used on him. Left out on the hill now for the crows and the ants and the blowflies.

There was footsteps outside.

Footsteps, up the steps.

I gripped the knife and squeezed my eyes shut.

I held my breath.

Cool air rushed in around me.

'What are you doing?'

I hid the knife behind my back.

'Why aren't you in your room?'

'Just getting the fire going.'

He eyed me, then the pot-belly.

'With the knife?'

He was breathing deeply, in and out, almost like he'd been running. Like he breathes after our running race. His sack looked heavy, and blood dripped on the timber floor in big dark spots.

I was embarrassed about being scared, and about the knife, but relieved too.

I was happy he wasn't angry. But mostly, I was just happy he was okay.

'Light the candles,' he said.

He carried the sack to the table, spilled it out. Big chunks of meat. Different this time, the flesh not as dark.

'Those bullets are rippers,' he said. 'They'll make life a lot easier.'

In the encyclopedia, goats look much nicer when they're still alive. They're a bit like sheep, but taller. Their skin in the pictures isn't like the ones he brings home. They're more woolly in the pictures.

I showed him once.

'Our ones are different,' he said, 'because they're wild.'

He said there are lots of different breeds, which is probably true. Like dogs.

It didn't say anything in the encyclopedia about that. Or about how smart they are compared to sheep, but I'm guessing they're probably the same.

He picked up a smaller chunk of meat.

'We'll have this one tonight. The rest goes in the pit.'

There were smears of blood on his pants and shirt. I don't think he's ever come back so dirty before.

'Did you see anything?' I said.

He went to the pot-belly, crouched down, and pushed the black sticks to the back.

'Like what?'

'A fire? From the smoke I saw?'

He got more dry twigs, cracked them in his hands.

'This is the only fire you need to worry about. And we need to get that meat on soon, or we'll be eating it for breakfast.'

Another time he answers, but doesn't really answer. It annoys me a bit.

'You've got to make sure there's enough air getting through. For a fire to burn properly, it needs oxygen. If the wood is too close together, it won't work. You should know that by now.'

I watched what he did, but it looked pretty much exactly the same as what I had been doing.

He pushed some dry leaves in underneath. He blew on the leaves, the flames licked up, and the kindling caught.

He smiled. Gold tooth.

I put the bone handle knife back in the drawer.

He went to the table, took the big knife and started working around the bone, his fingers deep in the meat. I wonder if he thinks about cutting off his fingers every time. I do.

'Steaks tonight,' he said.

The wind whistled outside and the candles flared.

Even though I don't like goat, I was glad we were having steak. It's much better than the roast.

He smiled. 'I've got a bit of a surprise to show you.'

He left the meat, went to the cupboard above the sink, and reached inside. The fire was crackling, it was cold out, and I was glad he was home. Even if he loses his temper sometimes.

'Close your eyes.'

I could smell him as he came close. It was different. Sweet somehow, but something else too. Like the pit, but not as strong.

'Keep them closed.'

'Okay.'

'Hold your hands out.'

It was cool and heavy and smooth on my fingers.

'Open.'

Slowly, I opened my eyes. Very slow, so it lasted longer. I stretched it out as long as I could.

It was a glass bottle with a white top. The label was torn, so I couldn't read what it was. Inside was a dark, thick liquid.

'Know what it is?'

I shook my head.

'It's sauce. For the steaks. I got it when I went to town, but wanted to surprise you. Made from tomatoes. Anyway, it's good stuff. Makes everything taste better.'

I tipped the bottle, held it to the light. The sauce was dark red, like blood. Darker than normal blood. Thicker too.

'We might grow some again. Tomatoes, I mean. If it keeps raining like it has. They need a fair bit of water. I think I've still got the seeds somewhere.'

'Sounds good.'

He smiled, gold tooth. His eyes looked good, better. Better than they have for a while. Maybe finding the sauce helped. Or scaring Christine off.

Both these things.

•

He was right about the sauce, it did make the steak taste nicer. It's hard to describe it. It's sweet, but salty at the same time, and so rich and delicious that I could hardly taste anything else.

'Don't use too much, try to make it last. We'll save it for when the meat isn't as fresh.'

I scraped off some of the sauce with my knife, put it back in the bottle.

Without the sauce, the steak wasn't that great, but still better than usual. Didn't need as much chewing.

'It's good,' I said. 'Not that it's bad normally.'

'She was a young one. Separated from its mother. Was lucky to find her.'

The fire was burning hot, almost too hot. I shifted back in my chair.

'Why'd you take so long?'

He took a while to answer, scratched his beard.

'The goats have moved further past the hill now. They must be looking for new spots to graze. It's further to walk, and further to carry it back.

'I'll show you sometime. But we'll do the practice in the next day or so, like I said. Give the rifle a go.'

He took my plate. When he turned, I slid my hand into my pocket.

Three good pieces, but no sauce.

Still, I reckon the fox will love it.

thirteen

At first, I thought I was hearing things. Or still dreaming. Do you hear things in your dreams?

I opened my eyes, but it was all pitch black in my room.

I heard it again.

Somewhere outside, maybe in the paddock.

I sat up on the edge of the bed. I thought it could be the fox, but it seemed too far away.

Maybe up the hill.

I went quietly to the window, moved the sheet. The moon was half out, soft silver light on the paddock, the trees.

There was nothing.

Then, I heard movement in the house.

I went out to the kitchen. He was there, his dark shape in the gloom. My eyes adjusted. He had the rifle, resting across the table.

I could hear the click of the bullets going in.

'Go back to bed.'

His voice was rough with sleep.

The hollow-points.

'Is it . . . ?'

'Just go to bed. It's nothing.'

I could tell from his voice that I had to do what he said. I went back to bed, pulled my blanket up to my chin. I listened as carefully as I could.

Steps down the hallway, the door swung open.

Crack! Crack!

Two quick shots out into the night.

He slammed the door shut.

Did he get it? Did he shoot whatever it was?

He went back down the hallway, heavy steps.

I tried to breathe more slowly.

He closed the door to his room.

After a bit, his door opened again.

Down the hallway.

My creaking door.

His breaths, in and out.

I was scared, but tried to hide it.

'You all right?' he said.

'Yep.'

'There's nothing to worry about.'

'What was it?'

'Probably wild dogs. I let off a couple of warning shots, just to scare them off.'

Wild dogs.

'Did you see them?'

He paused.

'They'll be off up the hill. So no need to worry, just go back to sleep.'

He stood there for a moment longer, and I could feel his eyes on me. He closed the door slowly.

'Goodnight,' I said, and I hoped he heard me.

He didn't answer.

fourteen

First light through the window. I pulled the sheet across and looked out to the paddock, to the sheep. They were bunched in the corner near the bottom of the hill. Still sleeping.

I couldn't hear my father snoring, couldn't feel him in the house.

I figured he probably went to check the traps again, to look for the fox's parents. Maybe the fox's parents have joined up with the wild dogs. Dingo too.

It was cold, so I put my jumper on. I got the fire going. I wondered what the porridge would be like with tomato sauce, but we have to save it for the steaks.

The leaves burned but the branches took a bit to catch. A bit green. That's how they are when they've still got moisture in them, when they haven't dried out.

I went to the window and looked out to the reservoir, to see if he was coming. In the corner of my eye, there was movement near the sheep.

It was him, climbing through the fence from the hill. The rifle was with him.

I gave the fire another go with some thinner branches. I didn't want to use too many matches, because they don't last forever. He gets the matches in town, but keeps most of them hidden away. Not because he's worried I'll take them, but because he wants to keep close track. He says once they run out, there's other ways to light a fire, but it's much more difficult.

We had a lighter once, and it was pretty great. It was blue and made of plastic with liquid inside, and a steel wheel on top which spun and made it flame. It didn't last very long. He said it was used for smoking, which he tried to explain, but I didn't really understand. He told me to look it up in the encyclopedia, but I didn't, mostly because I wasn't really interested. He said he'd look for another one in town, but never mentioned it again.

I tried blowing on the leaves, and the small twigs started to catch.

He opened the door.

The wind carried the smell of the paddock from outside. He closed the door behind him, leaned the rifle against the table.

'Cold out.' He rubbed his hands together. 'Just been checking the traps.'

He started emptying the bullets on the table.

'You ready to have a go? After breakfast, we'll have a few shots.'

The fire was going properly, and I was pleased. I was happy to have a shot with the rifle too, but a bit nervous. I didn't want to make any mistakes.

'Nothing in the traps?' I said.

He shook his head. 'Must've moved on, I think. Maybe they just wanted the lambs. Maybe the sheep are a bit big for them after all.'

I wonder why he didn't mention going up the hill, but I knew it was better not to say anything. Not now, anyway. I don't want him to know I was spying on him, which is what it's called when a person watches someone without them knowing.

I'm sure he's got a reason for not telling me where he went. Maybe he was looking for the wild dogs, to make sure they were gone.

He just didn't want me to worry.

•

He made me carry it from the house, get familiar with it. It's heavy, but I like the feel. How smooth the wooden bit is, and the thick leather strap which smells like sweat. Carrying it makes me feel older.

At the edge of the farm, below the hill, he set up two empty tins of baked beans on a fence post.

'I'll show you first.'

He took the rifle.

'We've got to take out the cartridge.'

He pressed a button, and the thin steel container popped out from behind the trigger.

'This is where we put the bullets. Takes eight in there. This one's a semi-automatic, which means you don't have to reload after each shot, but you have to pull the trigger each time. Make sense?'

He slotted the bullets in, one after the other.

'You have to give them a bit of a push, because there's a spring in the cartridge, which is what gets them in the chamber.'

I watched as closely as I could, because I knew he'd make me do it on my own after. I'd seen him load it before, but this time was different. And I wanted to get everything right.

He pushed the cartridge back in.

'Then you turn the safety off.'

The click of another switch.

'We're ready, more or less. So now I bring the stock up against my shoulder, like this. Just firm, not too hard. It's important to stay relaxed. If you get tense, you haven't got a hope.'

I looked at the baked beans cans. They sat there all quiet, not knowing what was coming.

'You have to line up the sights. That's the most important part, but everything's important. These two little notches along the barrel, you need to get them in a row, right in the middle, with whatever you want to shoot directly behind it.

'Now, once it's lined up, just squeeze the trigger slow. Don't pull it hard, because you'll throw your aim off. Just slowly, and keep your breathing nice and steady.'

I watched his breaths going in and out, slow and deep. He squinted one eye.

The gunshot echoed – the sound, so loud, again and again.

The two cans stayed where they were.

'Your turn now. Hopefully, you'll do better than me.'

He passed the rifle, my ears still ringing. It felt warm. I brought it up against my shoulder, like he'd shown me.

'Now, line them up.'

It was hard to keep it level, with the weight of it, and the wind blowing, and him watching so close.

'Nice slow breaths, okay? When you're ready, just squeeze the trigger, not too hard.'

It went off before I knew it, kicked back into my shoulder, my bones. Two crows took off into the sky from the bush behind.

I'd missed by miles.

He laughed. 'Those crows got a fright.'

He gave my shoulder a squeeze.

'You'll get better. Just takes a bit of practice.'

I looked up to the hill, the thick green darkness.

I passed him the rifle.

'Are you sure it was dogs?' I said. 'Last night?'

He cleared his throat. Clicked the safety back on.

'Reckon so. Most likely.'

'Couldn't be the others?'

He eyed me. 'Why would you think that?'

I shrugged. 'Or Dingo?'

'Dingo?'

'He might've come back.'

He laughed, but in a different way than normal. Not a proper one, which is from deeper down.

'Not Dingo. Not unless he's come back to haunt us.'

Haunt.

Haven't heard him say that word before.

He raised the rifle, lined the cans up again. He took longer this time, like he was really concentrating.

The shot went off and the can on the left disappeared altogether, like it was never even there.

'Bullseye,' he said.

He passed me the rifle.

'Five left. Let's see if you can get the other one.'

I didn't get the other one. All five shots. But he said we'll practise once a week from now on, instead of one of our lessons.

'Can't do more than that, only got so many of the old bullets. And I've got to save the hollow-points.'

'What happens if we run out?'

'I'll get more. In town.'

'What about when that runs out?'

He didn't answer for a while, and I thought he wasn't going to.

He looked up to the hill, then back to me.

'We'll have to get creative,' he said.

fifteen

S he didn't rush to the back of the cage this time.
   I caught her licking her leg, but she stopped when she
saw me.

Her eyes, they're hard to describe. You can almost disappear
in them, like there's a whole world inside of her.

I went slowly, tried not to frighten her.

I opened the door.

'Here, fox.'

Her eyes went wider, but she didn't come.

Don't think she could understand what I was saying.

I reached into my pocket and took out a piece of goat. It
had gone a bit grey overnight, but was still okay. It was a nicer
bit, I didn't want to give her a nervy piece.

Her ears turned, nose twitched, sniffing the air. She could smell it, I think. She wouldn't have had cooked meat very often. Suppose foxes don't cook their meat. They don't have a little kitchen down in their burrow or anything. Would be pretty amazing if they did, if they had different rooms like we do. A kitchen, bathroom, a school room, and bedrooms. Maybe they all sit at a table together and eat and talk about what happened that day, how the traps are cruel, and how delicious lamb is.

I put the meat in the middle of the cage, halfway between me and her. She looked at it, then at me. I stepped back, waited a bit longer, then went back further, behind an old drum, so she couldn't see me. I looked around the side and she moved slowly across the cage, stopping to lick her leg, then she stopped near the meat. She gave it another good sniff, then chewed it down all greedy.

It made me warm inside, in my chest. She must've been hungry.

I tried a second piece, just outside the door this time. She came more quickly, snatched it up without chewing properly. She coughed a bit, like it caught in her throat, then licked her leg.

'Good girl,' I said.

I picked her up carefully and took her out into the open. She walked in the grass, in the sun. When she gets bigger, and her leg is better, she'll run a lot faster. Most likely back to her burrow, her family. Away from us. Especially if she remembers how she got caught. If she remembers that, she'll definitely run away. But she'll have a good story to tell.

I haven't got much time to make her my friend, to get her to trust me a bit. I wasn't the one who put the trap there, not really, even if I was upset about the lambs. I've told her this.

I wonder what the sheep would do if I took her down to meet them. I wonder if they'd know what she is. The bigger ones, especially the old bastard, might attack her.

Maybe I can train her to be friendly to the sheep. Maybe, if she's fed enough, she won't be interested. I read in the encyclopedia once that dogs were used to herd sheep, so maybe foxes can too.

Herd is one of those words with two meanings, but different spellings, even though it sounds the same.

heard
perceive with the ear.

herd
number of animals, esp. cattle, feeding or travelling or
    kept together.
to assemble animals in this way.

I hope the fox will stay with us. Maybe once she's better, I'll take her down to the sheep.

•

I stayed up late as I could. Stayed up until he was snoring and all was dark. I listened as carefully as I could.

Nothing. No sound. No sign of the wild dogs. No sign of Dingo.

He must've got scared off by the rifle. Makes me a bit sad to think about it. He probably came to try to make friends with my father again, like Christine did.

It would have hurt him. In his belly, his chest. That's where things hurt the most.

I've got a feeling he'll come back, though. He'll come back and then maybe him and the fox can be friends.

It'll be perfect.

Maybe Christine will come back too. Christine might help my father be happier, if he gave her a chance.

I hope she comes back. If she comes back, the soft eyes might be gone for good.

I looked up what that word means.

He must have the same feeling too. Dingo might be back some time, just to visit.

haunt

(of a ghost) visit (a place) regularly.

sixteen

Three mornings in a row.

He thinks I don't know, but I heard him the first time. He doesn't realise the creaky boards talk. They tell me what's happening.

I didn't see exactly where he went, not the first time. Second time I did, because of the moonlight.

We watched him go out there, me and the moon, but not toward the reservoir. Not to check the traps.

Each time he had the rifle, but I never heard a shot. He doesn't take the hessian sack, doesn't take the knife either.

Maybe he's looking for the wild dogs. For Dingo. Or something else.

Each time he comes back before the sun rises, back before he thinks I'll be up. Normally, he'd be right about that.

Except for the creaky boards.

I stay in bed when he returns, pretend to be asleep. Second time, he even went back to bed himself, tried to cover things up. He doesn't sleep though, I didn't hear him snore.

It's all make-believe.

•

At breakfast, he asked me something. First time in ages.

'How's the fox?'

'Good.'

'Looking after her?'

'Yep.'

'How's her leg?'

'It's okay.'

He swallowed down the last of his porridge.

'No sign of any more,' he said. 'They must've gone.'

He stood up and looked out the window, as though he might see the family of foxes there, waving and saying goodbye.

'Reckon they've gone for sure. So hopefully, we'll get some more lambs. And no trouble this time.

'Don't know how many years the old bastard has in him, for breeding I mean. Hopefully, we'll get a male or two.'

It was the most he'd talked in ages, probably since we went shooting.

It makes me think about Daniel again. And Patricia and Rosanna. There's a burning in my belly, but not as bad as before.

It makes me feel bad too, but in a different way. Makes me feel bad that I don't care as much.

He wanted to cook one, but I've decided to pretend that didn't happen, that he didn't really want to. He was just talking, to show he was tough. He does that sometimes, I think, just to remind me how life can be pretty brutal. Something he's said before, more than once, like I need to be reminded.

'Might need to shear a couple of them,' he said.

'Why?'

'Jesus, how many times do I need to explain things to you?'

I didn't answer, but I don't think he'd ever explained it before. I'd remember.

'We can't have the wool getting too long, or they get dirty. Then the flies start to cause problems.

'They'll get flystrike, which is when the flies get in their arse and lay maggots.'

'Maggots?'

'Like baby flies. But they look like worms. Anyway, I'll need you to help me with the shearing.'

The flies and the arse thing sounds a bit disgusting, like it's a story he's made up, but there's no way I could say it.

He took a deep breath in and out.

'Listen, I'm sorry if I get in a bad mood sometimes. I've had a lot on my mind lately. I'll try to be better from now on.'

When he said sorry, it was strange. It was strange because it made me want to cry. It made me want to cry more than when he gets angry, which doesn't really make any sense.

'It's okay,' I said.

•

I looked up in the encyclopedia about flystrike, but there was nothing. Looked up about the maggots too, but there was nothing about that either. So I looked it up in the dictionary instead.

maggot
larva, esp. of the blowfly.

I don't know what maggots look like, so this is really just a guess.

seventeen

Ever since we got the fox, they're definitely acting strange. Not that the sheep have ever been really friendly, apart from the lambs.

We did the shearing today, and I noticed how they're different. They move away from me more now, like they're nervous.

The least friendly is the old bastard. Definitely. I wish he'd got killed instead of the lambs.

He's old, skinny, and with two long curly horns chipped at the ends. He has saggy balls swinging between his back legs. They're all crinkled and disgusting, and they make me feel a bit sick.

I probably shouldn't wish that he died, because then there'd be no one to breed with the female sheep and make new lambs. If the old bastard died, my father would get the soft eyes for sure. Or the man with the deep voice might come back. Maybe both these things.

He must've been really upset about Daniel getting killed, but not so much about Rosanna or Patricia. My father, I mean, not the old bastard. He must've been planning to eat one of those two, not Daniel.

I'm glad he didn't want to eat Daniel, even if it makes no difference now.

The old bastard is pretty mean, always grinding his old yellow teeth like he's got something in his mouth. He sees me as a threat, but it doesn't make sense, because he never gives my father a hard time. Or charges at him. But he did at me once.

It was probably my fault because I was staring. I was staring at him because of how he was looking at me, so he started it, and I couldn't help but look back. He was grinding his teeth and scraping his hoof against the ground, and I don't even remember seeing him running at me, so I must've blocked that bit out. That can happen sometimes, if you really don't want to remember.

The old bastard got me right in the ribs. I could see the sky, then the ground, then the sky again. My father said it was lucky I didn't break any bones.

'You were lucky,' he said. 'If he'd been younger, you would have got really hurt.'

Either way, I was pretty upset. Angry too. I don't think the old bastard has ever forgotten about it. I definitely haven't.

He took the shears from out of his back pocket.

'Bit rusty.'

It'd be better with electric shears, and much quicker, but no hope of that. He's told me before that's how they used to do it.

He's talked about electricity a few times, how it used to make machines work by themselves. I've never completely understood how it worked. Don't think he does either, because he couldn't explain it very well. He said something about burning coal, which is a rock from underground. I wasn't really that interested.

'They make it so it becomes like lightning in the sky. That's a kind of electricity too.'

He pressed the handles of the shears and they shifted across one another. They make a metal noise, like scissors, but rougher. They're not very sharp.

He walked through the sheep and found the one he wanted. He grabbed her, she called out, and the others took off across the paddock.

Sheep are funny like that. They stick together normally, but if one is in trouble, the others run. They don't hang around and stick up for it.

'Survival of the fittest,' he said.

I don't know what he means by that. Said for me to look up something called *Darwin* in my encyclopedia.

It was the mother, I think. The mother of Daniel he picked out. I can't be completely sure, but I think so.

'If we leave that, she'll be in trouble. You hold her.'

I stood in front, grabbed hold of her shoulders firm, but not too hard. She looked at me up close in the eyes. I wondered what she was thinking. He was clip-clipping with the shears round the back, but her eyes were on me. They're beautiful, strange, but gentle with big lashes. She pushed against me, like she wanted to run, but I held her firm.

'Keep her still. Almost done.'

I rubbed her head. She smelled like the cool air up on the hill, and there was something I could see inside of her. There was something sad behind her eyes.

'I'm sorry,' I whispered. 'I'm sorry about Daniel.'

'What did you say?'

'Nothing.'

He eyed me.

'All done.'

I let her go.

She trotted over to the others, and she looked cleaner round the back, the wool much shorter and whiter. The other sheep looked at her sideways, like they were unsure why she got picked out. It's like they weren't sure whether to trust her now, like maybe she's on our side and not theirs.

There's no sides though, not really. Our side is theirs, but they don't realise it.

'There's a couple more we'll have to do, but we can leave it for later. Might head up over the hill, just for a bit, to see if there's any goats around. Getting a bit short on the meat.'

Thing is, I don't really see how we're getting short. He got one only the other day, and it usually lasts for ages. Especially now it's cooler. And I've only been taking small bits for the fox.

I think he must be going up for another reason. Same reason he's been going in the morning. Maybe he's worried about more of them coming, ever since Christine came. More of them from the commune.

But I won't say anything. Not yet. Have to wait for the right moment.

Like I said before, *when* you ask something matters more sometimes than what you're actually asking.

Almost as much.

Sometimes, anyway.

·

The fox wouldn't come out of the cage this time. Wouldn't even come for the goat meat, which I put inside. Not even when I shut the door behind it. Might be because it's one of the bits that had sauce on it. Maybe.

So I went to the pit. I lifted the lid and held my breath, just for a few seconds, then I let some of the air through my nose, but not too much. It's not as smelly as it's been before.

I was surprised how little was left, compared to how much he brought in the sack last time. Don't think we've eaten that much, but we must've.

It made me feel sick, but I reached down and pulled out the last lump. I tore some of the meat, and it came really easily, like it's starting to rot.

Might be just as well he's gone hunting for more.

eighteen

My father cooked the last of the goat for dinner. He called it corned goat, which he's never done before. Cooked it in water, which took ages.

It didn't taste any good, but I know not to say anything. Still, it's better with the sauce, so I put as much on as I could.

'That's enough,' he said.

I wish he'd just chucked out that last rotten bit. He shot one yesterday, but hasn't cut it up yet. Wasn't a young one this time.

'That was a lucky one,' he said.

He put the new one down the pit and said we have to finish the old one first, because we can't afford to waste any. It's disappointing, because I wanted to get the new one to try with the fox.

She must be getting homesick – that's why she isn't eating. Must be thinking about her father and mother, back in her burrow. Maybe her brothers and her sisters too. Maybe she knows they've left the farm, and she'll never be able to find them.

Makes me sad to think she's feeling like that, alone out in her cage in the cold. I'd like to bring her inside, but I know he'll get angry if I ask.

•

I looked in the encyclopedia, like he said.

One was a city in a place called the Northern Territory, but I don't think that's what he was talking about. The other one is about *Charles Darwin*, which I think is the one he meant. Turns out the city was named after Charles Darwin, so he must've been a pretty big deal. A city is like a town, but bigger.

Couldn't really understand most of it.

He was some sort of scientist.

scientist

a person who is studying or has expert knowledge of one or more of the natural or physical sciences.

I still didn't really understand, so I asked him.

'A scientist is just someone who reads books a lot. A bit of a know-it-all. I knew one or two, back in the town.'

In the encyclopedia, it said Charles Darwin did some sort of experiment about animals which said the ones that survive usually have something special about them, and the other ones die.

'More or less right,' he said. 'Means only the strong survive.'

There's a picture of Darwin in the encyclopedia. He looks a bit like this.

I traced it.

We haven't had a lesson in ages, but I'm not so worried about that. I don't miss them really. Not much, anyway. I still go into the school room for the encyclopedias, and to practise my drawings on the blackboard.

We haven't had a lesson since he's been going up the hill so often. He's been different since then. Like there's something behind his eyes. Something he doesn't want me to see.

It scares me a bit.

nineteen

It's been too hard to write about, but now I think I can. It might take me a few goes, but I'll try my best.

If I'm honest, I probably knew it was happening, but pretended not to see. Part of me knew, but not all of me. That can happen sometimes.

It was when I last went out to see her.

I crouched down and she shrunk against the far corner. Her little chest puffed in and out. I reached inside, slowly, but she moved to the other corner.

'Shhh,' I said.

I took her in my hands. She felt warm. I took her carefully out of the cage, held her to my chest.

She shivered.

He watched, then slowly unwrapped her leg. The bandage was stained, crusted hard. Yellow and green.

She struggled against me, squealed.

I turned away.

'Look,' he said.

The wound was dark, smelly and thick with pus. Her leg was swollen double the size of the other one. Flies suddenly buzzed in. I tried to shoo them away, but they just came back.

He breathed deeply in, then out.

'Flystrike,' he said.

I never knew a fox could get flystrike. I thought it was only the sheep and their arses. He never said anything about it, and maybe he should've. Maybe we could have done something to stop it.

The fox squirmed against my chest, then relaxed.

'She's tired,' I said. 'She just needs to sleep. Maybe if she sleeps for a while, then she'll feel better.'

•

It was a long walk to the hill. Somehow, it felt longer than ever before. He didn't speak the whole way, his boots crunching the dry grass.

I held the fox in my arms. She liked my warmth, the slow, steady beat as we walked across the paddock.

She stopped shivering.

'That's good,' I said. 'She's getting better.'

He didn't answer, didn't turn back.

Her breaths were fast and shallow, her scent rich and sweet. I wondered if we might keep walking, if we might just go right up and over the hill. We could go on and through to the town. Me and him and the fox. Keep going, maybe forever.

To somewhere better. A place where things like this didn't happen.

We got to the fence, and I looked to the hill above.

He shielded his eyes from the sun, pulled the wire apart.

I climbed through carefully with the fox.

•

It was in the clearing, near the old creek bed.

I wondered if there was water in the creek, since it rained. Wondered if it washed away what was left of Daniel, Patricia and Rosanna. If it took them somewhere better, somewhere without the ants and flies and crows.

We never gave her a name. Thing is, I didn't really know for sure if she was a boy or a girl. She was always just the fox.

He took her from my arms. She yawned, like she was ready for sleep.

Tears stung my eyes. First time in ages. I squinted and kept them in, only just.

He cradled the fox, gently. She licked at her lips. Looked at me once, deeply, just before he turned. He went down to the creek.

It was dark and cool in the clearing, and I sat in the dirt, crossed my legs. Always cooler up the hill, mostly because it's shady, but the air is different too. Wetter, heavier, and feels different in my chest.

A magpie called and a mozzie whined at my ears. Must be water around, if there's a mozzie. Mozzies are the most terrible insects. It's not enough they drink your blood, and make you itchy, but then they have that awful sound too. Keeps you awake at night.

If you were going to make the most annoying insect you possibly could, the mozzie would be it. Plus, they might have helped spread the plague too. That's what my father tells me, but he's not completely sure.

I wonder how mozzies survive when there's no people around. If they drink the blood of other things then, maybe birds or rabbits or goats. Or even each other.

Maybe mozzies aren't the worst. Maybe it's the flies doing flystrike with their maggots. The maggots eating the fox's leg and eating the sheep's arses. That's probably worse. Especially the fox's leg.

My picture before wasn't right about the maggots.

They look like this.

I wonder if people can get flystrike too. If you've got a cut on your leg, maybe the maggots can get in there. Or in your arse.

Ants are bad too. Probably worse than mozzies, because they work as a team. They march in long lines and bite and take pieces of meat back to their hole, which is the nest underground where they all live. I don't think they'd have rooms or a kitchen like the fox's, all just down in their tunnels biting each other and being awful.

I once put a frog on top of an ant nest, as an experiment, and they all swarmed over it. The frog's mouth was opening and closing, like it was telling them to stop, or asking me for help, or maybe just asking why I did it. Then it stopped moving.

I've always felt terrible about that. But it shows just how bad the ants really are.

So maybe mozzies aren't the worst. Maybe something can seem bad, or annoying, but underneath it's not as bad as other things. Maybe people are like that too.

I kept trying to think about the mozzies, the flies, and the ants. But the fox and him down in the creek kept coming back. Not in my mind so much, but deeper down.

I could still see them, feel them in my chest. I wish I couldn't. Wish I couldn't imagine or feel things like that. He says sometimes how it helps to have a good imagination, but I'm not sure that's always true.

The wind changed direction, whipped cooler through the trees, and I lifted my knees to my chest. The leaves rustled and the branches creaked like they're tired of it all, like they were waiting for the night too, for sleep.

I closed my eyes as tight as I could.

I covered my ears and squeezed them shut, so nothing could ever get in.

So I wouldn't see or hear anything in the whole world, ever again.

But still, I heard.

•

The sun goes down quickly on the hill, in the trees and under the branches. I heard him first, but I had to squint to see him.

He was coming up from the creek, through the bushes, his face grey-blue in the gloom, the rifle across his shoulders.

There was something stiff about the way he moved, unsure. Like something had changed in him, but I don't know what.

I shivered from the wind. He came in slow, close, and pulled me up off the ground. He smelled of sweat and dirt.

He wiped my cheeks with his hands, squeezed my shoulders, and sighed long and deep.

I'm still upset at myself for crying, even if I did it silent. If you do it silent, it's not as bad. Still, I wish I could have stopped it.

'Can I see her?' I said.

He shook his head.

'Just for a second. Please.'

A deep breath, in and out.

'All right. Quick then.'

I went through the scratchy bushes, down to the bank of the creek. There was water there, but not much. A few puddles where the creek should be.

I went down a few steps, but not far. I could see her, curled on her side. She looked smaller. Her long, thick tail swooshed up beside her legs, her eyes closed in the deepest sleep. Sleep of the deepest, most lovely dreams. All the nice dreams you've ever had, all in one go that never ends. That's what I imagine it's like.

I went closer, down into the creek bed. Touched her once.

'Goodbye, fox.'

Her body was soft, her muscles relaxed. No flies, but I knew they'd come. The ants as well, and whatever else.

It won't matter then.

Or now.

Because now she rests. She sleeps. She dreams.

·

He walked ahead on the way back. Silent. Rifle slung over his shoulder, swinging lightly. Glad for its work.

The sheep raised their heads as we passed.

I felt angry at them, for the fox.

I wonder if they're pleased now, happy the fox is gone.

I try not to think of her, but I can still smell her. Feel her.

She's in the wool of my jumper, on my skin. I can close my eyes and see her. The place where she dreams – a warm cave in the earth, deep inside her burrow. Her father and mother, brothers and sisters.

Where she belongs.

She's there, I'm sure of it. And I wonder where I'll go, when it happens to me.

·

Once we were close to the house, he took the rifle from his shoulder. Clicked the safety. Turned to me.

We stood there for a bit. The wind whipped across the paddock, and he stayed like a statue in the falling light. Like a picture I saw once in the encyclopedia, of a statue on an island somewhere.

Like a stone that's been here, on this farm, forever. Who will, somehow, always be here.

He looked at me, eyes shining, black as pitch.

And he said something.

'Sometimes, you have to do the most terrible things. Sometimes, you just have to.'

That's what he said.

part three

one

L ast night, I listened.
I listened as carefully as I could.

I heard the wind rush down the hill, across the paddock, and the timber of the house creaked, almost like it was alive. The house was talking to the wind, talking about the past. It was telling the wind about someone who lived here once, and what she was like. How she looked after the house and the people in it. How she cooked nicer food in the kitchen. How she got sick and died a bad death.

All these things. That's what the house talks about.

And the wind talks about what's been happening in the paddock, up on the hill, and beyond to the town. The wind travels through all those places, so it knows, and it tells the house. It told the house about Christine and Jessie, about my mother on the hill, but the house already knew all these things.

The house isn't happy with me and him, and how things have been. It wishes my mother was still here. It wishes she was still here with her damper and the roast potatoes.

It was saying this to the wind. And the wind was saying we came from the town, and it knows all about us. It knows about Elizabeth Taylor. It knows some secrets too, but isn't allowed to say.

The creaking is the house wanting to move. It wants to get up and walk away from here, from me and him. Go up the hill and beyond to the town, where there are streets with houses it can talk to. The place the wind has told it about.

I listened hard to hear what the wind was saying. I concentrated and listened, hard as I could. I listened out for Dingo too, but there was nothing.

My father started snoring, loud and throaty, but I tried to block that out. I rolled on my side and faced the window, out toward the hill.

Then, I felt it. I felt it before I saw.

Up under my arm, my left arm, toward my back.

Breath caught in my throat.

I pulled the blanket off and sat up straight.

There was no moon, the room as black as it's ever been.

I moved to the edge of the bed. Tried to breathe.

Slowly.

More slowly.

I traced fingers up my side. Carefully, with my fingertips, because I thought I must've got it wrong. Must've just imagined it. It just couldn't be.

A lump. A small, round lump.

I pushed and it felt firm, almost like muscle. Didn't shift under the skin, like it's from somewhere deeper, further inside me.

I squeezed it, but it didn't hurt. It's like it isn't really part of me, like it doesn't feel a thing.

I went slowly to the kitchen. The fire in the pot-belly was almost out, a weak yellow light on the dusty floor. I was careful to miss the creaking spots.

The wind picked up again outside. Windows shook, loose iron clattered on the roof, and something fell in the steel and timber stacked in the paddock.

His snoring stopped. So I stopped and waited until it started again.

I felt my way slowly along the wall, the table, the kitchen bench. I found a candle, lit it. It flared as the wind whistled through the house and its secrets.

I shielded the flame with my hand.

From the secrets, from the wind.

•

The bathroom doesn't get used much, hardly at all nowadays. I think it got used more when my mother was here.

There's the toilet, but he turned off the water for that ages ago.

So there's not much need to go to the bathroom anymore, especially because we wash in the dam. The bathroom isn't a nice room anyway, cold and hard and creamy green.

But the bathroom has got one good thing. He uses it to shave sometimes, but not very often. Usually when the weather's hot. I've watched him do it a few times, and it takes forever. He uses scissors first, then a long steel blade he scrapes across his skin. It has a name, but I can't remember it.

I put the candle on the edge of the sink.

My ribs poked out a bit, more than I remembered. A bit like my father. I looked skinnier, and there's hollows in my cheeks, but maybe it's my imagination. Your eyes play tricks on you sometimes. Like your ears. That's what my father tells me.

I raised my left arm, turned my body.

I brought the candle closer. It's almost like a bruise, but I definitely didn't bump anything. I'd remember if I did.

Maybe it was the mice. He said people thought the plague came from rats, but maybe it's mice too.

'It's one of the worst ways to die,' he said.

People tried to cure it, but it didn't work, and it just kept spreading. The plague, I mean.

'They started rounding them up. They got taken somewhere, never came back. So people kept it a secret.'

That's what my father tells me.

He stopped snoring. There was movement in his room, I could feel it.

I went back down the hallway, fast as I could. I closed my door gently.

Outside, the wind picked up again, whispering to him what the house had seen.

'You'll have to deal with it,' the wind said. 'Deal with it soon. It's not something you can just leave be.'

But I'll keep it a secret.

From the wind, from the house.

And from him.

two

L ast night, in the dark, I stayed awake. I stayed awake and
I listened again.

I listened to see if he might come, if he might call to us.

He might come back, now the fox is gone.

He would have got confused before. Might have thought
we got another dog, especially after he fired the rifle at him.

He would have smelled the fox, even from far away, but
might not have known what it was.

Dogs smell things much better than people can, that's what I
read in the encyclopedia. They can smell things from miles away,
and hear things too. They can smell things about a thousand
times better, which is why the police used them as sniffer dogs,
which is what the encyclopedia had a picture of.

The police were the people who told other people what to
do. He told me about them in a lesson once. They don't exist
anymore.

Smelling things a thousand times better than normal would
be good for a while, but probably terrible too. Especially with
things like the goat. Or things that are rotten. Or the sewer.

I'd be able to smell the goat in the pit, even when the lid
was on. I could smell the oily sheep in the paddock, the rabbits
in their burrows. The dead fox in the creek.

I stayed awake for as long as I could.

And I heard it.

It was outside.

The paddock. The hill.

In the wind and the creaking it was hard to tell, hard to
be sure.

I went to the window, because your eyes can't be tricked.
Not like the ears. Not as easy.

There was no silver moon this time, and nothing I could see.

So I listened.

It was different this time, but I'm sure I heard it again, below
the wind.

Lower, softer.

But it wasn't like he said.

It wasn't a wild dog, I don't think.

Wasn't Dingo either.

It's something else.

three

My father took a long time to get up. I don't think he was asleep, because I couldn't hear him snoring.

I didn't say anything. I waited to see if he might, but he didn't.

He must know I heard.

Must know I heard him, heard him rush from his room. The door swing open, the crack of gunshot out into the night.

He must know.

He went out early this morning too. He went up the hill with his rifle, then was back before sunrise. This time, he took the hessian sack. It looked like he had something inside it when he left, something heavy, but it was hard to tell. But I could tell it was empty when he returned. He went back to bed, pretended like he'd never left.

Once he was up, he cooked his porridge himself, not saying a word.

But I could see it behind his eyes. I could tell, because he wouldn't really look at me.

It was hiding there, just waiting for me to say something. To say the wrong thing. To say I saw him. To say I knew.

To ask what he's been doing.

It was hiding and trying to catch me by surprise.

It was just waiting for me to ask.

I didn't.

four

My father still hasn't told me where he goes. Hasn't said a word about it.

But he said something strange this morning, when I asked a question. First thing I've asked him in ages.

It happened in the kitchen, after I made his breakfast. I asked him because I checked his eyes first. I thought it was safe.

'Can we do something for the fox?'

He didn't answer.

'Could we do the same thing? The thing we did for Daniel?'

He stirred his porridge.

'The funeral we did? Can we go up there?'

He looked at me.

'You go.'

'Me?'

'Yes.'

'On my own?'

He shrugged.

'I've got things to do, but don't be long. Check the fence on your way. A couple of posts look a bit rotten.'

He's never let me up the hill on my own. Never with his permission, anyway.

'Too risky,' he'd always say.

But there's something different about the way he's talking. It's not like the soft eyes, though. It's different. It's not like the anger either.

It's like the words come out, but I can tell his thoughts aren't the same. His thoughts aren't the same as his words.

It's hard to explain.

Maybe it's a bit like what he does with me sometimes, how he can see my thoughts through my eyes. I can't see his thoughts, not exactly, but I can tell they're different than normal. I can feel it.

I'll try to explain it better sometime.

But I can't write more about it now, because I have to go up the hill.

I have to go before he changes his mind.

•

She looked almost the same as we'd left her, but it's hard to know what's underneath. What's underneath her fur. Maybe underneath there's maggots, but I tried not to think about that.

You can never really know what's underneath things. Like the rusty sheets and the mice. Like him and his eyes.

There was flies, but the ants hadn't come. Maybe ants don't like foxes, like it's not their thing. But from what I've seen, with the frog and the lambs, they'll go for pretty much anything.

I tried to put something else in my mind instead, the only way to stop thinking about it. If you just try to force things out, they nearly always come back. Sometimes, they come back bigger and worse than before. Especially when you're in bed, because all you can do is think then.

I said two prayers for the fox, the *Hail Mary* and *The Lord's Prayer*, which is the proper name for the Our Father one. Then I said them again, but the other way around. If I say them more, it might give her a better chance of getting where she needs to go. To *Heaven*, even if I don't believe in it, or maybe to the place of dreams.

I tried to find a new prayer in the encyclopedia, something special just for her, or special just for foxes, but there weren't any. I've asked him before if he knows some. He said there are lots of different ones, but I'd need a book called *The Bible* for it, and he's never had one. He said some people in the commune had *The Bible*.

'That was part of the problem.'

I didn't ask what he meant by that.

It'd be good if there were prayers just for animals, and special ones for different types of animals. Maybe it's something I could write myself.

The first one would go like this.

Dear Fox,
What happened wasn't your fault
But we couldn't let your family eat our lambs
We don't think you did it
You would have been friendly to the lambs, if you'd known them
You were a good fox
Smart and gentle
Even if your life was short
I won't forget you
So, in a way, you get to live forever.

I said it out loud, and it didn't sound too bad, even if I hadn't written it down first. I think it made me feel better than the other prayers did. Probably didn't do much for the fox, but maybe the others don't do much either. Maybe they're just meant for us people left behind, to make us feel better.

But this time, after I said the prayer, something happened.

The sound cut through the trees – went right inside me.

It stopped my breaths.

I listened.

The same, I think. The same sound I've heard. But I was closer.

It was coming from somewhere further up, further up the hill.

I didn't move. I kept still like the fox. I kept listening.

I could hear the rustle of the leaves in the trees. I could hear birds talking to each other. I could hear the hum of the earth below my feet.

I listened, and I waited a long time.

But there was nothing more.

I reached down and stroked the fox's head.

'Goodbye, fox,' I said.

I left the creek and the fox and went back to the trail. I looked up to where it winds further up the hill, where the trees and branches come in closer.

I imagined going further and further up, the trees closing in, dark falling around me. I imagined turning back and the trail had gone.

The trees would scratch and claw if I went there, try to keep me forever.

Then the others might come. Like he says they would.

I stood there a while, too long, wondering if I should. If I should go find where the sound is coming from.

A magpie called from down the hill, it called and said to come back down. It's seen what's up there. It's seen it, but won't say what it is. It won't say, because it knows saying things makes them more real.

But my father knows, that's what it says.

He knows what's there.

And sometimes, he comes.

five

It's hard staying awake all night. I've only tried once before, and I didn't make it.

It was a long time ago, and I'd wanted to see if the others came like he'd said. I watched through the window for ages, but sleep came over me like a warm and heavy blanket. I didn't even notice it happening.

But I was younger then. This time, I'm better at it.

I heard my father rise. His bed whined and sighed, like it was happy to be rid of him. There was no wind outside, and the house didn't creak. It was going to help me this time, not tell any secrets.

I heard him move across the floor of his room, then heavier in his boots. He stepped slowly down the hallway and into the kitchen. It was still dark, but he knew the way. Every bit of this house, the farm, everything. In darkness and in light.

I sat up and moved to the edge of my bed. It squeaked a little, so I stopped, waited to hear any reaction, any shift in his movement. I slipped on my socks, my shoes. It was cold, so I wrapped the blanket around me.

I didn't hear the front door open. He did it carefully, because he doesn't want me to know. My bedroom door shifted slightly, and I felt the chill on my skin.

I checked the window first. There wasn't much moonlight, but the stars shone brightly enough. Bright enough to see his shape moving across the paddock. The rifle looped over one shoulder, hessian sack on the other.

He told me about the stars on a walk once, but I never understood. He said they're not in the same time as us, but thousands of years in the past. They're like bright explosions a million miles away, and we can only see them now.

'They're so far away it takes thousands of years before we see them, so what we're seeing is actually thousands of years ago.'

That's what my father told me.

It's one of those things where he knew I didn't understand, and he couldn't say anything to make it clear. He just smiled and roughed my hair with his fingers.

It's been ages since he's done that.

But it made me think. It made me think that if we're seeing them thousands of years ago, they'd be seeing us in the same way. So they wouldn't actually be seeing us, but whatever came before. They'd see before we came to the farm, back to when we were in the town. They'd see us in the commune. They'd see before the plague and before us. Before the others.

If you went out to those stars, you could see back into the past, to before we even existed. I'm not sure how you could get there, or even if it's possible.

'People use stars to guide their journeys,' he said. 'Especially sailors out at sea.'

I wonder if Sirena does too. If when she's catching the tuna fish, she uses the stars.

'The stars would tell the sailors the way home, so they'd never be lost.'

Before my father told me, I'd always thought the stars changed every night, that they were in different positions. I never knew it was always the same.

I watched him head toward the hill. He's a bit like a sailor, but without the sea. I wondered if maybe he uses the stars in the night sky to guide him to the same place. The place further up the hill where the sound comes from. Where the smoke comes from too.

Whether the stars guide him to whatever waits there. Whatever waits for him, his rifle, and the hessian sack.

But I know it isn't just stars that bring him back home, that guide him back to the farm.

'Always lean a stick against a tree, so you don't get lost. So you know which way you came, which way is home.'

He taught me that in a lesson.

•

I was careful not to get too close, but I was close enough to see which way. Through the fence, onto the trail, away from the paddock and the stars.

The sheep stayed near the dam as I passed. Some slept, while others kept watch, which was different than normal. Maybe since what happened with the lambs and the fox.

Two turned to look at me. They would have seen my father each morning, gotten used to it by now. But they must've wondered where I was headed. What trouble I was looking for.

It was harder once I was on the trail, heading up the hill. I had to get close enough to see which way he went, but not so close he could hear. The further up the hill, the narrower the trail. More turns, more decisions. He didn't use the sticks every time.

He moved steadily, his shoulders angled through the branches closing further and further in. The skin was torn on my arm, I could feel it, but I didn't make a sound.

Somewhere in the trees, a currawong started a lonely call, but there was no answer. It must've been confused by us being there, thinking the sun was up. Maybe it was talking to me, giving me a warning like the magpie did. Telling me to go back down.

I went past the turn where my mother is, then the clearing near the creek bed, then the fox. I couldn't see him anymore, but I could hear his steps on the wind. The dry leaves and twigs under his boots, a cough like something had caught in his throat.

I went past where we collect the firewood – it all looked so different in the dark.

The air was cold in my chest. The wind picked up and swayed branches into my path. I turned back to see where I'd come from, but it was hard to tell. I listened for his steps, but there was nothing but the wind in the trees. There was no turn-off, so I knew he must be ahead.

I went on more quickly, my heart beating stronger. The trail narrowed, it winded and turned, circling the hill.

I couldn't see him.

I stopped and listened. I listened as hard as I could, hoping for something out there. Maybe he'd gone off the trail, somewhere through the bush, a place only him and the stars know.

I looked to the sky, hoping for something. The stars stared at me from a thousand years in the past.

Then, that sound.

I felt it as much as I heard it.

In my chest, my belly.

It was coming from further up.

I kept going up the trail, pushed through the branches, the thorns.

I heard it again.

Closer.

I came to a fork, a path left and right – both ways into darkness. No stick. I looked to the stars again. A thousand years ago they would already know, already know about this place. About the farm and the hill. About us.

I went left, and the trail soon disappeared. I could've turned around, headed back down the hill, but I went on. I should've gone back, gone back while I had the chance. Gone back before I saw, because some things are better not to see.

I was in thick scrub, stepping over dead logs, and the twigs crunched under my feet. I came to the creek where it still runs. I could hear the water trickling between the rocks, but there's not enough to make it further down.

I stepped carefully on the rocks, then up the bank and through a row of tall, thin trees.

I was cold, bleeding, and lost.

I wished for home. I wished I'd never come up here. I wished for the fox, and for Daniel. I wished for my mother.

Then, I saw.

I saw it in the corner of my eye.

Shining through the blue gloom, from between the trees.

White, slick skin.

Her hair pulled back tight.

And him.

.

Her wrists were tied together with rope, her mouth covered with cloth. He held her hair with his right hand. He was in close, talking in her ear, but I couldn't hear a word.

She nodded. Her eyes wide. She didn't make a sound.

Her skin was pale and hair almost white. She was tall, taller than me, but not as tall as him. I couldn't say how old she was, but older than me. Somewhere between me and him.

Christine.

I wanted to hear her voice, to hear again what she sounded like. If it's what I've been hearing in the night.

She was wearing something strange. Tight blue pants and a bright orange jacket, zipped up to her neck. Her boots had laces all the way past her ankles. She looked dirty.

I saw a chain shift across the dry grass. It was looped around the trunk of a tree, and her ankle. The chain from his cupboard.

I crouched down lower.

You'd never find the place if you didn't know about it. You'd have to have been there, or followed him like I did. No one would ever go there, unless they had a good reason.

Aren't many reasons, I don't think.

But he goes there.

For Christine.

And his reasons.

I watched and listened, but was too far away to hear his voice. He was downwind, on the slope from where I was hidden. I moved to a tree that was closer.

It was risky. If he spotted me, I didn't know how he'd react, but I knew it wouldn't be good.

He was still talking. His mouth moved, his hands too, out in front of him. Like he does with me sometimes. Like he was explaining something important, something complicated.

He looked different than normal. His face darker, deeper shadows in his cheeks. I could almost imagine him being someone else. If I squinted my eyes, it could be his brother, living up on the hill, who we never see, and he never talks about. His brother who's done this, who's chained her up. The man with the deep voice.

What I tell myself.

He went to his hessian sack and reached inside. He took something out. It looked like goat.

He went to her, held it in front of her face. He pointed at it, and she turned away. He brought it closer.

He reached behind her neck, her head. He untied the cloth from her mouth. Deep breaths in and out.

She didn't speak.

He brought the goat close again, she shook her head.

He took her hair, brought her face forward, the meat to her mouth.

He smiled. Then stroked her cheek.

She chewed, spat it out.

My chest thumped hard, so loud they might have heard. I tried to calm myself, to slow my breaths.

He brought the meat up again.

She faced up toward the sky and its first hint of blue. The night was about to end, the sun was coming, and those stars a thousand years ago could sleep.

She bit again, properly. She chewed and I could almost feel the gristle crunching in her teeth. The blood and tendons, her tongue twisting back against the taste.

He let her go. Touched her hair gently, brushed it from her face.

He said something to her.

He pointed at the rifle, leaning against a dead grey stump. She swallowed.

I wanted to go closer. I wanted to know for sure that it was Christine. I wanted to know why he has her chained.

I looked to the sky again. The stars were gone but a slice of the moon was still there, like it must've been hiding behind a cloud. Hiding from all this.

I didn't feel tired. My whole body was all nerves and electricity, like the lightning in the sky.

•

The magpies began their call. The morning call, that's what my father calls it. He told me about it once, on one of our walks.

'Just letting each other know they're alive. That it's still their territory. All in order, and as it was.'

I had one last look, so I'd remember.

Her strange clothes, the meat in her mouth, her eyes so wide. The things I saw.

•

Everything looked different going the other way.

I wondered if I'd made a wrong turn and was going down the other side of the hill, toward the town. I went faster, hoping I might see something, something familiar, or one of his sticks. But the trees looked the same everywhere I turned.

Then, suddenly, I was in the clearing near the creek bed. Near the fox. The lambs.

I stopped and caught my breath. I squatted down.

Other birds had joined the chorus, so I knew I didn't have long. When they all join in, the sun is close.

That's what my father tells me.

•

I closed my eyes, but sleep wouldn't come. Light seeped into my room, through the sheet.

It was later than normal. He'd stayed longer.

Eventually, I heard steps outside. The crunching grass. The door.

He went quickly to his room, quietly as he could.

But I heard.

And I waited.

I waited til he came out of his room, down the hallway. Tap running, but not the kitchen. The bathroom.

He hardly ever goes there.

Water ran. Splashed. A noisy rattle in the pipes. Then he went to the kitchen.

I sat up on the edge of the bed, took off my pants. I felt for the lump under my arm. I put on my pyjama pants, then my jumper to cover the scratches on my arms.

'You're late,' he said.

He was crouching down in front of the pot-belly, trying to get the fire going. His hair wet, slicked back. He'd washed his face, his neck.

I sat at the table, pretended to yawn.

'Tired?'

He arranged the kindling.

'Didn't sleep well?'

I shrugged. 'Had some dreams.'

He lit a match. 'What sort of dreams?'

I shifted forward in my chair.

'Can't remember, not exactly.'

'Was I in them?'

He gave me a sharp look, but I couldn't read it.

'I don't think so.'

Flames licked from the paper underneath the kindling. He stood up.

'About the farm?'

'Maybe. About the sheep, I think.'

The fire took hold, and he got the porridge pot from where it lives, under the bench. I squinted and tried to see the man on the hill, his brother. The man with the deep voice. He looked different, even if he's definitely the same.

He had scratches on his arms. Must've got them on the trail, like me.

'Sometimes, dreams are like real life.'

He dusted his hands on his pants.

'Dreams can be about things you wish you could do in real life, but can't. Freud said it, I think.'

He scooped some oats into the pot with his hands.

'F-r-e-u-d. He'll be in your books. Look him up.'

I tried to remember some real dreams, not the made-up one about the sheep, to see if he's right. I remembered one about my mother. It was something I'd wished for, but it didn't come true.

I was trying hard not to think about the woman on the hill, chained to the tree. Trying hard not to think about it, so he couldn't see my thoughts.

I can't be sure it's Christine, but it must be.

I wonder how long she's been there, and how he caught her. I wonder why he has her chained. I wonder what she does during the day, then at night.

She must be scared about things coming.

Wild dogs. Foxes. The others.

Or maybe she is one of the others.

There's a lot I don't know. I know more and less than I've ever known, all at once.

I felt for the lump again under my arm, through my jumper. He filled the pot with water, put it on the fire. He looked at me and smiled. Gold tooth.

There was something different in his eyes, but I couldn't say what. Not exactly.

He stirred the pot.

'You'd be surprised about your dreams,' he said. 'Sometimes, they come true. Sometimes they do, whether you like it or not.'

six

It used to rain more when the seasons changed.

The days would get shorter, the nights much colder, and it would rain.

Now, the dark clouds come. They come from over the hill and I can tell my father's watching them, even though he's trying to look like he isn't.

He's watching them and hoping for it, but it never seems to happen.

•

It was after breakfast, he said it.

'Might head down to the dam later. Need a wash something terrible.' He sniffed. 'So do you, I reckon.'

He roughed my hair with his fingers.

'I'm all right,' I said.

'Don't argue. You're coming.'

•

I took off my jumper, my t-shirt. I couldn't see the lump without the mirror, but I could feel it.

I tried putting my arm over it, bent a little so the elbow protected it. I figured it might work for a bit, until he wants to inspect me. Wasn't sure what to say about the scratches. Maybe I tripped over somewhere.

But he knows what the lumps look like, that they're different from a bruise. There's no dark colours, no yellow, purple or green.

I've tried to make it go down. I pressed on it, but it sprung back like it's been there forever.

I'll run away until I figure things out. Up the hill, maybe around the other side and toward the town. I don't know what I'd find there. Or how long I'd last.

He always said there's only one cure for the plague.

The rifle.

So I'll have to keep it a secret.

I looked up the encyclopedia like he said. It's got something in there, but it's all too hard to understand. I found the bit about dreams and it sounds like what he was saying, but I can't really be sure.

I'll draw a picture, to take my mind off things. That works sometimes.

That's what he looked like. He'd be dead now, I think, but I don't know if he died from the plague. He's a bit like Darwin, but with a smaller beard.

I traced some of it. I couldn't do it that good on my own.

•

My father stripped off first, which he always does.

He threw his pants on the muddy bank, not far from me. The bones in his back remind me of a lizard I saw near the big dam once. The lizard was small and spiky, and he told me it was a mountain dragon. I've never seen one since.

I undressed slowly, carefully. As slow as I could.

More time. Let the sun go down. Let it get darker.

He was already in the water, arms crossed to the cold.

'Beautiful in.'

He laughed, and his *Adam's Apple* went up and down. The *Adam's Apple* is the thing in his neck that pops out sometimes. I don't have one.

I've looked up before about the *Adam's Apple*, and it was something about *The Bible*, which has the prayers. There was a story about an apple that someone called Adam got stuck in his throat.

I've asked him about it, and he said it's like *Heaven* and *Hell*. Like the stories people use to get you to act in a particular way. But he didn't really tell me much about it, the story I mean.

He took a deep breath, his belly sunk in and his chest puffed out. He dived underneath, disappeared, and small waves washed up on the bank.

You wouldn't know he was there, slicing through the muddy water, somewhere deep under the surface. I've never gone fully in like that, even when we've been swimming with the rope. I ducked my head once and it was dark underneath. I didn't like it.

I shouldn't say it, but part of me hoped he wouldn't come back up. Part of me hoped he might stay there forever. It scared me a bit.

I moved around the bank, to the side where the hill is, where the sun is too. I figured, facing the sun, it'd be harder for him to see.

He broke through the surface, wiped his face with his hands, coughed and spat.

I took off my undies, slowly.

'Gone shy?'

He smiled. Gold tooth.

I stepped slowly down the bank, my arm bent, holding the washcloth, covering it with my elbow.

The water was freezing.

'Warm, isn't it?'

He laughed, but it got caught in his throat, strangled by a shiver.

I tried to wash myself, tried not to touch the lump. But I couldn't help it. The more I tried not to think about it, the more I could feel it. Things are like that sometimes.

He washed his hair, his eyes closed. I knew it was nearly the end, because it's always the last thing he does. I wondered if I should just tell him. Maybe if I was honest, it would make things different.

He moved into shallower water, near the bank, up to his knees.

'C'mon, come have a quick look before we freeze. I'll head back and get the fire on. We'll have steaks tonight.'

He lifted his arms, turned his body. Nothing but slick, smooth skin. His hair flat and wet.

No lumps.

'Your turn.'

I kept my arm bent, turned around. I felt the cold water on my skin, the mud between my toes, the wind whipping across from the hill.

I felt him look me over.

I waited for him to say it.

'Lift your arms.'

I closed my eyes and held my breath.

'Jesus,' he said. 'Too bloody cold, let's get out.'

I took a deep breath. The air was cool and sweet in my chest.

He must've been distracted.

Maybe it's the woman, Christine, from the commune. Up on the hill.

Maybe he was thinking about her.

I dried myself quick, got dressed.

The sun was almost gone, but he waited for me.

The sheep looked up as we passed, then headed back to the dam. They were waiting for us to leave so they could get back to their favourite spot.

We walked across the paddock, and I could feel a tingling in my legs, my arms. It was relief.

Then, near the house, he stopped. He turned to me, crossed his arms.

'Listen,' he said.

He eyed me, took a deep breath in and out.

'You know what I'm about to say, don't you?'

My chest went tight.

'No.'

'You must know.'

'Know what?'

He uncrossed his arms, took my shoulders in his hands.

'I'm not blind.'

Tears stung my eyes, but I kept them in.

'It's okay,' he said. 'I'm not angry.'

'You're not?'

'You should have just said something.'

'I know.'

'I was expecting you to.'

He looked past me, through me. He was seeing something I will never see.

'I know that hill,' he said. 'I know it so well.'

His gaze met mine.

'I saw you there.'

I swallowed. Tried to speak. Nothing came.

'On the hill. In the bushes. I saw you watching.'

'I wasn't—'

He touched my shoulder, squeezed it.

'C'mon,' he said. 'It's too cold out here. Let's go inside.'

seven

My father waited til after the steaks were cooked. Until we were eating. We used the last of the sauce and it was delicious. It covered the taste.

The pot-belly banged and cracked, like the wood might be green. He leaned back in his chair, hands behind his head. He looked happy to be clean and warm by the fire.

'What do you think?'

'Good. But I wish we had more sauce.'

He smiled. Gold tooth.

'Nah, what do you think of her?'

My face went hot.

I didn't know what he wanted, what he expected me to say. It took me a while to think of it.

'Is she the visitor? Is she the one who came?'

My chest thumped hard. Was sure he could hear it.

'Nah, that bitch is long gone. I found this one up on the hill. Got lucky.'

I used my finger to gather up the rest of the sauce. The sauce is salty and sweet on its own. More sweet, I think. Sweeter at the bottom of the bottle.

I tried not to look at him, so he wouldn't see my thoughts.

'She must've got separated,' he said. 'From the others, I mean.'

The others.

'So she's . . .'

He nodded. 'One of them.'

The sauce was all gone. Nothing left. And there was nowhere to look but the fire.

When it's really going, the flames lick up the sides and it's like they're alive, dancing around each other. You can squint your eyes and imagine them like that, like little monsters.

She was nothing like I imagined the others would look like, but I couldn't say it. Nothing like Larry Hagman, or the devils I'd drawn.

'Bit of an experiment,' he said. 'To see if I can train her.'

'What about the plague?'

'What about it?'

'Couldn't she have it? Or be a carrier?'

He shook his head.

'I've checked her over. And she might be able to help us on the farm, if things work out. But you're not to go up there, not without me, all right? The others will be looking for her.'

He reached over, opened the door to the pot-belly a bit wider, gave the fire a poke with his foot. It crackled and flamed, his face yellow-red.

'I'm teaching her a few things. To get her ready, you know? If she comes here. It'd be good to have a woman's touch again. You wouldn't remember, but your mother made things nicer. More like a home.'

There was a flicker in his eyes, like he saw my thoughts.

'Don't worry,' he said, 'I'll look after her. And it's all gonna be different from now on, I promise.'

eight

Sometimes, my father says things in a way where I know not to ask questions, a way that closes things off.

His mouth tight. The anger hidden behind his eyes. I know now that's nearly always the thing he's hiding there.

'Get the sack,' he said. 'And come with me.'

I didn't ask questions.

I walked beside him. He had the rifle and his knife, so I wondered if we were going hunting for goat. We haven't practised shooting for ages, but I hit the tins twice last go.

We went toward the hill. Then he turned toward the small dam, where the sheep usually drink and have their meetings. I still wonder what they talk about when we're not here. If they make jokes about me and him, about what's been happening

on the farm. Or tell stories about things gone before. What the
wind tells them.

They'd probably like to be running the place someday. Have
their own farm with grass and dams, and just stand around.
Things sheep do.

But the sheep weren't there this time. They were near the big
dam, which he's stopped checking since it's barely rained lately.
So it's the big dam again, not the reservoir anymore.

The sheep watched us. They watched us going to their normal
spot, like they were suspicious.

'Here,' he said.

In the dry yellow grass, before the edge of the dam. One of
the sheep was on the ground.

The old bastard.

Much worse than the lambs this time.

He was almost completely torn in two, from between his
back legs to his neck. The flesh was gone from his head, scraped
back to pink-white skull. His eyes looked at me, all surprised.

His guts spilled out on the grass, covered in flies. His guts
looked the same as the lambs, but there was more of them.
Even when you're old and different on the outside, the insides
look the same.

His front leg, the left one, was missing. Torn off at the
shoulder.

I felt bad for him, but not as bad as for the lambs. Probably
won't miss him that much. Still, he didn't deserve it.

The other sheep looked on. A few chewed the grass, like nothing had happened. Maybe those ones didn't like him much. But I've got no real idea of what they're feeling, or what they saw.

I don't feel as sad for the old bastard, but some of the other sheep must have liked him. They let him breed to make the lambs, so he must have had some good parts to him. Maybe he was gentle with them, even if he didn't like me so much. He was Daniel, Rosanna and Patricia's father, so he couldn't be all bad.

'The foxes?' I said.

He lifted the old bastard's head with his boot, like he was looking for clues underneath.

He shook his head. 'Someone's sending a message.'

I'm still not sure what he meant by that.

He looked up to the hill, just for a second. I wondered if he was thinking about the woman. Or the others. There was nothing in his eyes which told me. I still can't see his thoughts as clear as he sees mine, even if I can see the anger.

'Will we take him to the creek? Away from the farm?'

He shook his head. 'Doesn't matter so much now. We'll leave him here. The crows can pick him clean.'

He turned to where the rest of the sheep stood. A couple eyed him, shifted their position, moved in tight. The rest looked away.

'Not much point anymore,' he said. 'Not much use for the rest of them. Without him, we can't breed them. No more lambs.'

He pushed the old bastard's neck with his boot.

'That was the point, to get things sustainable. So we might as well make them useful now, before the meat gets too tough.'

He walked toward the other sheep, and I followed.

I tried to think of something to say, because I got a bad feeling. I got a really bad feeling like something terrible was about to happen.

The sheep moved a few steps, then held their ground. He stopped, brought the rifle to his shoulder.

It happened so quick.

The shot rang out across the farm, into the hills, and echoed somewhere beyond.

The woman would have heard it. Definitely. Maybe the others too.

All the sheep ran toward the fence, except one.

She didn't make a sound. Her legs kicked out a few times, then went still.

He stepped closer, the rifle in his hands. He turned back to where I stood.

I was scared.

I wanted to run.

'C'mon,' he said.

I went to him, legs shaking, hands too. I tried to hide them under the hessian sack.

The sheep's eyes were still open, blood in the wool of her neck and belly, pink bubbles out of her nose.

She breathed in and out fast.

He held the rifle out.

'You do it,' he said. 'Do her the favour.'

My chest thumped hard, the rifle heavy in my hands.

Her eyes rolled toward him, then me.

She was wondering why he'd done it, and why I'd make things worse.

The other sheep looked away, knew what was coming.

I raised the stock to my shoulder, felt the steel of the trigger against my finger. I lined the sheep's head in the sights. I closed my eyes, squeezed and—

'Wait.'

He took the rifle from my hands.

'It's a waste of a bullet.'

He pulled the big knife out from his belt. The silver blade, its handle black and worn.

'This way.'

He placed the knife in my hand.

'Go deep, but do it quick.'

The sheep looked at me. Kicked her legs.

I crouched down, slid my hand under her head. Her wool was warm and soft. I placed the blade against her neck. Blood pumped hard in my ears.

'Go on.'

He said it soft, like he didn't want her to hear.

Her breaths stopped, eyes frozen. Her stomach sunk.

She fell still, her pink tongue hanging loose from her mouth.

He sighed.

'She beat you to it.'

I stood up, dropped the knife.

'She'll do for now,' he said. 'We won't do any more today.
We'll do them as we need, so they'll last through winter.'

I looked across to the other sheep.

'You'll get plenty of chances.'

He looked at me, read my thoughts.

'You have to do these things sometimes. Have to toughen up.'

He smiled. Gold tooth.

Then he picked up the big knife.

And went to work.

nine

I didn't tell my father.

I didn't tell him, because I didn't want him to think I was happy about what happened.

But it was moist and salty and better than the rabbit. Not gristly like the goat.

Nowhere near as terrible as the goat.

Still, I felt bad. I felt bad that I liked it. It'd been ages since we'd had it, and it was even better than I remembered.

And I knew what he meant, about the old bastard. He explained it again, just so I understood. The idea was to get enough sheep so we could slaughter a lamb sometimes.

'Then we wouldn't be so reliant on the goats. Because when we run out of bullets, it's gonna get harder.'

It all makes sense, I know.

'I'm trying to do what's best. What's best for us.'

I nodded. Still, I don't really like the idea. Making lambs just to eat them. But we can't do it anymore anyway.

'What do you think?' he said.

'It's okay.'

'Just okay?'

His eyes widened when he said it. Like a question he didn't really need an answer to.

'The lamb would be better, of course. This is mutton. Old sheep. It's tougher, but the taste is just as good.'

I never knew meat had different names, depending on the age.

He chewed on a bone, wiped his mouth with his sleeve.

'The most tender is when the lamb hasn't started walking. Used to be able to get it back in town, at the butcher.'

Butcher.

I've never heard that word before. I wonder how they'd do it, how they'd get the lamb before it started walking. It'd be pretty awful.

When I was done, and my plate was clean, I asked.

'What about her?'

'Who?'

'The woman.'

'What about her?'

'The mutton. Will you take some to her?'

He picked up my plate. His eyes searched me, my thoughts. He couldn't see them, not this time. I was careful.

'Maybe,' he said. 'But I'm getting her used to the goat first.'

'What did she normally eat? Before, I mean.'

He shrugged, put the plates in the bucket.

'Where will she sleep?'

'Sleep?'

'When she gets here.'

'We'll work it out later. It's still a way off. With her training, I mean.'

I asked him what he was teaching her.

'All sorts of things.'

'Like what?'

He eyed me.

'You're asking a lot of fucking questions.'

His eyes scared me a bit, the white parts, but I tried not to show it.

'Practical stuff. Like, I'm gonna teach her to clean herself properly. She's pretty filthy, like most of the others. To be fair, it's probably because of her hands being tied up. But I can't risk having her loose. Not yet.'

I nodded, tried to show I was okay about it all.

'Now I think about it, I could try the mutton. As a reward, if she's doing the right thing.'

I was happy about this, but tried not to show it.

'You just wait,' he said. 'It's gonna be great. Like the sister you never had. Like having your mother around again, only better.'

I didn't like him talking about her like that.

My mother or the woman.

But I didn't say anything.

•

When my father talks about the farm being sustainable, he means making it so we can stay here forever. So we'll have enough food and water, and never have to leave.

I'm not sure I want to. Stay here forever, I mean. But I could never say anything to him about it.

It'd be nice to see other places, maybe, like the town. Maybe even places in the encyclopedia. Places like New York and Sydney, with big buildings. Places like the sea and the desert. It'd be nice to see them in real life.

With the old bastard gone, it doesn't sound like it can ever be sustainable. So maybe we might see those places. Maybe if Christine comes back, she might persuade him.

But I doubt she'll come back. He must've said something pretty nasty to her, for sure. Would've scared her off for good.

I looked up those places again in the encyclopedia, just to remind me, because there's some excellent pictures.

There was another thing I wanted to look up, but it wasn't in the encyclopedia.

I found it in the dictionary. There's a few different meanings.

butcher
person who deals in meat.
person who slaughters animals for meat.
brutal murderer.

None of them sound very good.

ten

A while since I've written. Haven't felt like it much anymore.
It's been days like this. Maybe weeks. Longer.

Seen the sun once or twice, but no warmth.

The farm feels smaller. The house too.

The weather has closed in around us. The cold. Clouds are
dark and heavy, but still no rain.

He's staying in bed longer now.

The soft eyes. They've come back.

He's not angry as much anymore. I haven't seen the whites
of his eyes for a while. In some ways, it was better when he was
angry. It's better than the soft eyes.

Neither are good, but the soft eyes are worse.

The soft eyes are like he's giving up, like he just wants to
live inside himself from now on.

It's hard to explain.

eleven

There's been no lessons for ages.

But I still go in there, the school room. I even practise my times-tables, just so I don't forget. Just in case the lessons start again and my father wants to test me.

He's spending more time up the hill now, less on the farm. Now I know, he's not so careful about it. Doesn't go up so early anymore.

But he tells me to stay in the house. My room. And he leaves me the big knife.

'Just in case,' he said. 'In case anyone comes.'

'Like who?'

He doesn't answer. But I know he's probably talking about the others. Or maybe Christine.

I hope she comes back.

The Others

Truth is, I don't know what I'd do if anyone came.

But he won't let me go with him up the hill, he won't let me see the woman.

'You won't hurt her?' I said.

He didn't answer.

But when he's been up there, I've heard her.

Maybe it was a bird.

Or the wind.

Maybe I didn't hear anything at all.

Things I tell myself.

twelve

Now it's cooler, the mutton lasts for longer. But my father still goes hunting goats in between.

'For every two goats, we'll have one sheep. You can do the next one.'

He said I'd have to kill the next one, then went off and did it himself. He must've forgotten.

I was pretty happy about this.

I didn't go with him, didn't even watch. I stayed in my room and looked at the magazine, tried to put something else in my mind.

Elizabeth Taylor. The woman on the hill. In that order.

Still, I heard it.

In some ways, it's worse not seeing things. It's worse because your thoughts paint the picture.

I could see the sheep's head coming apart, the skull splitting and flesh peeling back. The blood leaking out from behind her eyes. The other sheep watching.

Him smiling. Gold tooth.

I feel sad for the sheep. If we had more rabbits, it'd be better. But even rabbits are nice when you see them up close.

Anything you know, it's much harder to hurt.

•

I asked him something today.

'Why can't we shoot the birds instead?'

He eyed me.

'What's your problem with the birds?'

I shrugged.

'Magpies are okay. Currawongs too. But I don't like the crows so much.'

'They'd be the last ones you'd want to kill. Crows are smart, remember? One of the smartest birds there is.'

And I do remember what he said about crows. He told me on one of our walks. He said they're clever and loyal, and have just one mate for all their lives. One husband, one wife.

But I wonder what he meant today about them being smart. Like, maybe only things that aren't smart deserve to die.

So goats mustn't be smart. Same with the sheep and the rabbits.

But it's hard to know any of these things for sure. The sheep could be talking about really clever things among themselves.

We can't understand their language, but it doesn't mean they're not smart.

Same for the goats and rabbits.

•

I've seen a few more fires. More smoke. Not from our pot-belly, but up on the hill.

Three or four now, some close and some further away. Haven't seen the fires themselves, just the smoke. Grey and silent snakes in the sky.

I haven't said anything to him, but he must know. He must've seen them too, but isn't saying.

The old bastard.

The fires.

They're coming closer.

It's about the woman, I reckon. They're looking for her. Or maybe Christine knows about the woman, and she told the others.

She told the others about what he's done.

What he's doing.

He said he'd look after her. But I'm not sure he's telling the truth anymore.

Even less than normal.

thirteen

L ast night, I waited.
    I waited until I heard him snoring.

I was careful.

The flame almost went out a few times, but I protected it with my hand. The wind was blowing hard outside. I went slowly, missed the creaky boards outside his room.

His snoring stopped for a second, so I did too.

I waited.

I was careful.

He started again, so I went on.

I looked different than last time. Heavier, not as skinny. Must be the sheep, the mutton.

I angled my body so I could see.

It's still there, but hasn't got bigger. If anything, it's gone down. It's hard to be sure, but that's what I think.

I don't feel any different, and I'm not sick or anything.

If I could look in the medical book, I might find it. But the medical book is in the cupboard, in his room.

I don't want to go in his room.

•

I looked in the encyclopedia.

I don't know the names of things that might cause it, and it's hard just using pictures. Takes ages.

I found something though, a photo. In the A book.

It's someone's face, but it says it can happen on bodies too. On backs and other places.

Acne.

It says it doesn't cause major problems, except to people's *confidence*. It doesn't look like it kills you like the plague, or that it's contagious. If that's what it is.

There's a few different meanings in the dictionary.

confidence
firm trust.
a feeling of self-reliance or certainty.
something told as a secret.

This is a picture of the acne from the encyclopedia. And one of my lump. Side by side.

The Others

I've decided it's probably the third meaning in the dictionary, because it's a secret.

I don't have many secrets. A few, but not many.

Some secrets can be helpful, though.

Some things, they need to be secrets.

fourteen

My father was up early. But I was too.

It was cold, and he hadn't lit the fire. There was no porridge.

I could see dark circles under his eyes.

'I'm heading to town.'

He said it before I asked.

The rifle was leaning against the table. He picked it up and looped it over his shoulder, hanging loose at his side.

'We're short on bullets. We'll need them for the goats. It'll be a long winter, and we don't know what else is coming.'

He got the big knife out of the drawer, passed it to me.

'Stay inside.'

He turned for the door. I thought to say something about the fires I'd seen, to be careful. But I'm sure he must already know.

Maybe it's why he really needs the bullets. For what else is coming.

He stopped at the door, turned to me.

'You'll come next time. I reckon you're ready.'

I smiled. I tried to make him happy.

Truth is, I've always wanted to go to the town – I've always wanted to see the place where my father and my mother came from. The houses and streets. The shops. More than anything, I want to see the shops where you get tomato sauce and the oats and cans of Sirena tuna.

'That'd be great,' I said.

He smiled. Gold tooth.

He's going to take me, but not this time.

It was good he didn't want to take me this time.

I'm glad he wanted to go on his own.

·

The sheep watched me. And for once, I was happy they can't talk. Even if they could, I'm not sure they'd say anything. Whether they'd tell my father what they saw.

They're more loyal to me, I think. They'd be on my side. I haven't been shooting them, and I'm always nice to them. Up until recently, anyway.

Still, they must know what we're eating. They'd be able to smell the cooking. But it doesn't change how they act so much. They carry on like normal. Maybe a bit more nervous when he goes near, but I could be imagining it.

There was fog up on the hill, higher up. I crossed through the fence, and a crow called out.

Craaa-craaa.

It called to me.

It said to hurry, that there isn't much time.

I feel bad for saying we should shoot them. They'd have their own families and things like that, so shooting them would be cruel. All the same, I don't like them much. Not as much as the currawong. I think the currawong is probably my favourite.

There's always a risk he might come back early. It's only happened a few times, and not for ages. Still, the sooner I was back, the better.

I went quickly up the trail, because I mostly knew the way. But I put sticks on a few trees, just in case.

I got to the turn-off. I haven't been to see my mother in ages, and I feel bad for it. I stopped for a second, said a quick prayer. *The Lord's Prayer.* I remembered most of it, except for the bits about bread and evil. I remember those bits now.

I got to the firewood place, then further on to where the trail becomes more narrow. The bush is thick there, and the trees different – lower and more prickly.

I squinted my eyes and tried to imagine him up ahead, which way he went. Should've been easier in the daytime. It wasn't.

Then, I heard.

I stopped, waited for it again.

Wasn't far away.

I went more slowly, tried to be as quiet as I could. It didn't take me long.

She was on the ground, her back against the tree. Her hands were tied, but to the front this time, between her legs.

Her clothes looked dirtier in the daylight, her blue pants black at the knees. There were brown spots on her jacket, her cheeks red from too much sun.

At first, I watched her from a distance, from behind a tree. She didn't move.

She stared straight ahead, twisted the rope on her wrists. Her skin looked raw there. She frowned, gave up, reached for the cloth in her mouth. She tried to get her hands behind her head, to where the knot must be. She could almost reach, but her fingers were at the wrong angle, her wrists tied too tight.

She got tired, put her hands back to her lap.

Fast, shallow breaths.

I wonder if he ever cleaned her, or showed her how, like he said. It didn't look like it.

Craaa.

The crow called again from down the hill.

She closed her eyes.

I wasn't sure what to do. I hadn't really planned anything. I just wanted to see first, then decide.

I looked around behind me, where the trail led back down the hill. He'd be a while yet. Definitely.

That's what I told myself.

In the clearing, my chest thumped. I went closer to her, her white hair matted with dirt. Quiet steps, softly as I could.

Closer still, in front of her, her eyes still closed.

She looked smaller than I'd thought. Skinnier too. Her cheeks sharp angles, skin wet with sweat. Shallow breaths going in and out.

'Christine?' I said.

Her name came out before I could stop it. I put my hands in front of my mouth, tried to catch what I said, put it back in.

Her eyes flashed open.

She pushed her body against the tree. Stood up, staggered, eyes wide. She shifted her weight on one leg, mumbled something.

'It's okay,' I said.

My voice sounded strange, like someone else's.

I held my hands up.

'I won't hurt you.'

She shook her head, and I moved closer. She looked scared, and I wondered what he'd told her. What he'd said about me.

She tried to run, but the chain ended quick. She fell, arms out in front.

She didn't cry out, but lay there – her breaths going in and out.

'I'm sorry,' I said.

I could see the chain on her left ankle, the dull steel.

Crack!

Gunshot. The rifle. It didn't sound far away.

She twisted on the ground, onto her side. I could tell she was scared. I could feel it.

Scared of the gunshot.

Of him.

And me.

I backed away, slowly.

'I'll come back,' I said. 'I'll come again another time.'

But I don't really know if I will. I don't know if I should. And I don't know if she wants me to.

I stopped at the edge of the clearing, looked at her one last time. She was trying to stand, but her leg looked sore.

I could have helped her, helped her stand.

Crack! Crack!

Two more shots. Closer.

The farm. The shots sounded like they were coming from the farm.

I had to be quick.

Down the trail I went, the air whistling in my ears.

I've never run so fast, my breaths deep and rough, catching in my throat. The trees a blue-green rush.

Out of the bush, I came to the fence. I climbed through, but the wire hooked into my shirt. I pulled hard and felt it tear. I stopped for a minute, leaned on a post. I caught my breath.

The sheep were in the far corner, beside the big dam. There was nothing and no one else around. Nothing, but the house and the things that surround it. The barrels and timber, the loose iron sheets.

But there was something different.
I couldn't tell what straight away.
But something had changed from before.
Just a feeling, at first.
Then, I saw.
The house.
The chimney.
Smoke.

fifteen

The way he was angled.
His body.

His eyes.

I can't explain how, not exactly, but he looked strange. Not like his brother on the hill, but closer. His voice came from deep in his chest, then out through his teeth.

'You just don't get the fucking message, do you?'

Arms across his chest. Black hairs, blue veins, thin bands of muscle.

'Where have you been?'

I couldn't look him in the face, not at first. The whites of his eyes.

'To see my mother.'

He said nothing for a second. Longer.

'That right?'

'Yep.'

My gaze met his. A smile at the edge of his lips.

'Your mother?'

I nodded.

'To say a prayer for her.'

'And you had to do that today?'

'I was quick.'

Telling part of the truth helps. The feeling. Makes it easier.

'Really?'

'Yeah.'

'You were quick, were you?'

'Yeah.'

He smiled. No gold tooth.

'And you didn't go any further?'

'Further?'

The fire crackled.

'Up the hill.'

My face went hot.

Arms again. Black hairs. Veins.

Can't let him see.

'Why would I?'

Gold tooth. White eyes. He was scaring me.

'Oh jeez, I dunno. Visiting someone?'

I shook my head.

'Just to her grave, I promise. I came back when I heard the gunshots.'

He took a deep breath in and out.

'That the truth?'

'Yep.'

'You sure?'

'I'm sure.'

He shook his head. He stared at me, through me.

'If you ever leave me . . .'

He didn't finish what he was saying. I didn't ask.

I tried to fill the silence.

'I thought you were going to town.'

He sighed. Unfolded his arms.

The whites were gone.

'Changed my mind. Weather was closing in, so maybe tomorrow.'

He swallowed. *Adam's Apple* up and down.

'I knocked off a sheep on the way back. Was hoping to get away with one shot, but she wouldn't give in.'

I feel bad for the sheep, but was glad he was talking normally again. Glad he'd stopped asking me questions.

'You can give me a hand after lunch,' he said. 'We'll bring her back to the house.'

•

My bed's been moved.

The floor is dusty, and there's clean squares where the legs were before.

Before it was moved.

Only a tiny bit, but I can tell.

So I'll have to find a different place now. I had it between the mattress and the frame, but I can't be sure he doesn't know. I can't be sure he hasn't seen it. Hasn't read the things I've written.

If he has, it's too late.

I don't like keeping so many secrets, but I'll have to from now on. I don't think I've got much choice.

He'll know too much. He'll know about the acne and the woman. Mainly the woman. And he'll know what I've been thinking, not just from looking at my eyes.

He'll know what I'm feeling too.

•

I carried the hessian sack, him the big knife.

The sky had gotten darker, like rain was really coming this time.

I know it wasn't the real reason – the weather has never stopped him before.

He wanted to see what I'd do.

It was a test.

A test to see if he could trust me. That's what I think.

And now he's seen my diary, but he's keeping it a secret.

She was on her side, her eyes closed. Blood soaked her chest, where he'd got her first. What didn't kill her.

He looked at me. Read my thoughts.

'I took the first shot from a way off. Tried to make it more interesting.'

The flies buzzed in heavy, all around us. How do they know? How do they all come in so quick, and where do they come from? They must have a home somewhere. It must be terrible.

Her head was covered in them, black and green. Where the next shots went in, probably from up close. Her jaw hung loose, by skin and nerves and not much else.

Maybe he put the barrel in there, pulled the trigger. But I can't believe he'd do that. It's too awful.

He started hacking at her throat.

'Head's no good,' he said. 'Not good for much. Only a little bit of meat there.'

Her head wobbled while he did it, like she was nodding. Agreeing with him.

Yep, he's right, the head's no good.

'Some people used to eat the brains. They called it lamb's fry. They'd crumb it, but it was really fatty. Your mother cooked it once.'

He pushed in harder with the knife. Steel on bone. I could almost feel it.

'Watch close. You've gotta learn this stuff. You've got to get between the vertebrae. One day, when I'm gone, you'll have to do it. You'll have to do it whether you like it or not. So it's best to do it properly.'

The head rolled loose to the side. He sliced through the last of the tendons and skin.

'There,' he said. 'First bit done.'

'What'll happen?' I said.

'With what?'

'When you're gone.'

He dropped the knife at his side, wiped his hands. His eyes went a bit soft, his voice too.

'Well, this'll be your place then. You'll have to run things. And you'll have to look after it, for as long as you can.'

He looked up to the hill, then back to me.

He's seen the smoke too. Definitely.

'What about the woman?' I said.

'What about her?'

'What'll happen to her?'

He shrugged.

'She might be here. Helping. We'll see.'

'What about the others?' I said.

'What about them?'

I wondered if I should say it.

'They're coming, aren't they?'

He picked up the knife, wiped the stringy meat and blood on the grass. It took him a long time to answer.

'As long as we've got the rifle, they'll keep their distance. But you'll need to be ready.'

I tried to imagine being on the farm with the woman.

Christine.

Her eyes and the gag in her mouth. Her legs chained and hands tied. I tried to imagine her without those things. With a smile like my mother, clean and dressed fancy. Like Elizabeth Taylor in the magazine.

He went back to the sheep, sunk the knife deep in her shoulder. I almost expected her to cry out, but remembered she was dead. Her head was right there on the grass.

'I can ask her, you know.'

He didn't look at me when he said it. Just kept going through the skin and flesh, opening her up. Like a jumper on the wrong way, inside out.

The knife was sharp, liking its work. He held out the leg with one hand, gripping the ankle, went deeper into the joint.

'Whether you went up there. If she saw you.'

He put some weight on the leg, tried to loosen it from the shoulder. It cracked and squelched, dark blood oozed from within.

I should tell him. I should tell him the truth. I should tell him everything.

No more secrets.

'I didn't go,' I said. 'She didn't see me.'

He stopped his work, wiped the blade on his pants. Eyed me.

'You sure about that?'

I thought about this diary, thought about what he might do to make her tell.

'Yep, I'm sure.'

I was worried about the anger. The whites of his eyes. The knife in his hand.

He watched me.

A second, longer.

'Fair enough.'

I breathed out slow.

I was relieved. I was able to say it without giving away the truth. I lied, and it wasn't so bad.

I've never lied to him like that before. I've kept secrets from him, like the lump, but that's not the same. It's easier to keep secrets than to say a lie out loud.

He went back to the leg and it was almost completely loose. He hacked at the last few bits, the tendons holding it there, keeping it in place.

'The bag,' he said.

I passed it to him.

I know now. I can lie without him realising. Or at least until he finds out, which he won't.

I don't think she'll tell. It's just a feeling, but I'm pretty sure.

But I'll need to keep this diary really well hidden from now on. I've got a new spot. It's much better.

He definitely won't find it.

sixteen

Early this morning it woke me, just as the sun was coming up.
A low sound, deep.
Getting louder.
Thunder.
But louder than normal thunder.
I could hear it, then feel it too.
In my bed, in my room.
I was scared.
The window rattled, the house was shaking.
The house didn't know what it was, and it was scared too.
He came in.
He came in and his eyes looked worried.
'Stay there,' he said.
'What is it?'

He went to the window, pulled the sheet across.

'It's nothing.'

But it didn't sound like nothing.

It was loud, very loud.

'Way off,' he said.

He said it mostly to himself.

Sound travels slowly.

What he's said before, in a lesson.

Must be something a long way off. It must be a long way, but I can tell he's worried.

I could see his thoughts through his eyes this time.

Could see his just like he sees mine.

seventeen

He left early, like he always does. Before I'd finished my breakfast.

He looped the rifle over his shoulder, rolled up the hessian sack.

'I'll take you another time. I need to be quick. Get the bullets, and come straight back.'

He'd seen my thoughts.

'Stay in the house. I mean it. It isn't safe now.'

Must be about the others, why it isn't safe. About the others and the sound like thunder. Both these things.

He's been looking up to the hill more often too. The worry in his eyes. He's trying to hide it, but I can see.

That's why I asked.

'Is it because of the thunder? Is that why it isn't safe?'

'Thunder?'

'The sound. It was like thunder, but—'

He slammed his fist on the table.

'Don't worry about that fucking sound!'

The whites of his eyes.

I was scared. Tried to hide it.

His deep breaths, in and out.

He doesn't want to talk about the sound. Or the smoke. Or the woman.

Those three things.

He went to the door, stopped, turned back.

'If anyone comes, I want you to hide.'

'If who comes?'

'Anyone.'

'Where?'

'In your room. Under the bed.'

He doesn't know my plan about hiding in the water tank. I haven't told him.

He went to the kitchen drawer, took out the big knife. Placed it on the table.

'Keep it with you. Just in case.'

I looked at the blade. It made me think of the sheep. The blood.

'And put the board up across the door.'

His eyes had gone all shiny, like he was doing what I do sometimes. Like he was trying to hold something in.

He took a while to say it.

The Others

'We'll have to leave here soon. Sooner than I thought. It's not safe anymore.'

'Okay,' I said.

He shook his head.

'I've never wanted to leave. I told your mother I never would, no matter what.'

He went out the door. It was the last thing he said to me before he left.

Now I think about it, I should've said something. I should've said something more before he went to the town.

I don't really know what.

•

I've never left the farm, not properly. Only been as far as the hill.

I know my father and mother came from the town, and the commune, but it's nothing I can remember.

Not sure what we'll take. The rifle, definitely. The big knife too. I'll try to take this diary, if I can, so I can write down all the things we see, the things I've wanted to check.

The widow's walk, the town, and other things.

I'll take the *Women's Weekly* with Elizabeth Taylor. So I don't forget. So I don't forget what she looks like.

I don't know where we'll go, but he's probably worked that out. There'll be houses along the way, empty houses we can stay in. We might be camping – he told me about that once on a walk. He said we might go camping one day, up over the hill. We never did.

Before my father and mother came to the farm, they used to camp in a tent for holidays. Holidays are what you do when you're not working, when you don't have things like the sheep or the crop.

That's what my father tells me.

tent

portable canvas etc. shelter or dwelling supported by poles and cords attached to pegs driven into the ground.

A tent mustn't be very big, because it's portable. It means you can carry it around. I'm not sure if it can fit two people, but it must. Three might be hard, though.

Can't imagine he'll leave her up the hill, not after all the training. But I can't be sure.

It'll be a tight squeeze, but he must have thought all of it through.

We'll light fires to keep warm at night, and hunt for rabbits.

What I tell myself.

We'll be like explorers. My father told me stories about explorers when I was younger. Like Burke and Wills, who got lost and died. But then there were some who didn't die and went on adventures and found new places to tell the others about.

I don't think we'll take the sheep with us on our adventure. We'll probably just let them go.

If we let the sheep go now, the small dam might last a bit longer. There's barely enough for us to wash in now, which I don't mind so much. And my lump has gone down a bit more, which is good. I can barely feel it.

The plants next to the big dam are all almost dead, brown and thin. Not even the rabbits are interested anymore. He hasn't been asking me to water them, and the water there is pretty low too.

The dams. The sheep. The crop.

All these things aren't really working anymore.

It's not his fault, though. A lot is just bad luck. The bad weather too, the drought.

He's worried about the others, the smoke on the hill, and that sound.

Maybe that's all because of the woman. Because of Christine.

But it's the farm too. It reminds him how things didn't work out, even if it's not his fault.

It reminds him of my mother as well. That she's not here anymore. He used to say that. A long time ago.

He still misses her, I think.

Things haven't worked properly for a long time, probably since she's been gone. When we leave, he'll be happier. He'll smile more, like he used to. Gold tooth. He won't get the soft eyes, or not as much. He won't be as angry.

Things I tell myself.

But I'm waiting now. I'm waiting to make sure he doesn't double-back. Doesn't do what he did before.

I don't think he will, though. He knows I won't go again, because he caught me last time. He taught me a lesson.

Don't want to get caught. Not again. Definitely not.

eighteen

A while since I've written. Hard to find the time.
    Have to be careful.
It's dangerous now.
But I'll start with that day – with the last thing I wrote.
When he said he was going to town.
For bullets.
That's what he told me.
I'll write everything as best I can.
Everything I can remember.

•

I took the board off, but the door wouldn't open. I pushed as hard as I could, but it just wouldn't move. So I had to climb out my window, and then I saw what he'd done.

A barrel on the top step, hard against the door.

To stop anyone coming in.

To protect me.

That's what I thought.

I think different now.

·

In the clearing, leaves crunched under my feet, and I hoped he was far away.

I hoped he wouldn't see, or hear.

On the ground, her back up against the tree, just like last time.

Her head was low, hair down over her face.

I went closer.

'Hello.'

Her face stayed down.

'It's me.'

She looked up. And she made a sound, a sound like one I've heard before. The sound I first heard in my bed.

'Shhh,' I said.

Wet earth. Smoke. Sweat.

'I won't hurt you.'

I said it soft, soft as I could.

She stood up, pushed her back against the tree. Kept her right foot up off the ground. Eyed me.

She mumbled something.

'We're going soon,' I said. 'We're leaving the farm. So I don't have much time.'

Her eyes went wide.

'I'll help you. But you need to keep quiet.'

She mumbled again, then pointed at the cloth in her mouth.

'I'll undo it. But you have to promise you'll be quiet. You promise?'

She nodded.

She lowered her head, let me reach the knot, her hair oily under my fingertips.

The knot was tight, and I wasn't sure I could get it loose. I should've brought the knife.

'I'll make sure he takes you. You'll come with us.'

She tried to say something, and I could feel the warmth of her breath through the cloth.

I breathed through my mouth, quietly, so she wouldn't notice. My fingernails bent and it hurt so much, but the knot started to loosen.

Her lips were cracked deep, thin lines of dry black blood.

A bird screeched in the trees. Another called back.

'Help me,' she said.

She said it low in her throat, then coughed.

'Who are you?' I said.

Her eyes were red. Deep, dark rings beneath.

'Are you Christine?'

She opened her mouth, closed it.

'Are you one of them? The others?'

'Help me, please.'

Her voice was soft. Different than mine or his. Or Christine's.

She held her hands out to me.

Her wrists.

The rope had torn through her skin, the flesh bright and burning. There was a dark yellow crust at its edge.

I started on the knot, my chest pounding hard.

Her breath felt so hot on my skin.

I looked at the chain on her leg, her ankle. The padlock. The other leg was swollen, down near her foot. Red and purple. Dark blotches on her skin.

The rope came free, and she touched her wrists gently.

She pointed across the clearing.

Not to the trail, or up the hill.

In the middle of the thick, stunted trees, there was an opening. A gap that'd been forced, low to the ground.

Tears suddenly ran down her cheeks.

'What is it?' I said.

'He hurt her. I think he's hurt her.'

'Who?'

'My mum.'

'Your mum?'

A shiver went through me.

'Jessie? You're Jessie?'

'I've been trying to call out, but she couldn't hear me. Go look, please.'

It was a small, narrow opening, like an animal might use. You wouldn't even know it, wouldn't realise it was there.

There was a sound from somewhere in the bush, down the hill.

I turned and listened, but nothing more.

'Please!'

I didn't think that she'd get me in trouble, not on purpose.

Because then it'd just be her.

It'd just be her and him.

I didn't think she would.

•

The path was narrow and dark. I couldn't see far ahead.

I found a branch on the ground, a thick one. Just in case.

I turned back to her.

She pointed again.

I went on.

Dark soil like night, grooves worn into the soft earth under my feet. Like something was dragged there, something heavy.

I pushed through the branches, and rain started to fall like mist. It made me worry, made me think he might come back.

The trail got narrower, more uneven under my feet. A smell, low and wet. Sour in my mouth, on my tongue.

Something shifted in the grass, and I gripped the branch tight.

I wondered if she might be imagining things. She'd been chained up so long on her own. My father coming to her.

I'd read about it in the encyclopedia once, when people can't think properly anymore. They get put in places called asylums, away from everyone. When they can't tell what is real and what isn't. I asked my father about it, and he said sick people get sent there. He said they go there to make them better.

I heard something back in the clearing. Steel on steel.

I stopped, listened.

Nothing more.

The smell got stronger, and I breathed through my mouth.

A low humming noise, up ahead.

The trees thinned, darkness lifted.

A smaller clearing. A dead-end.

Blowflies.

They were everywhere.

Where they live, where they come from. The place I imagined. But different than on the farm, thicker in the air.

A crow walked the ground, yellow eyes. Unsure whether to leave. He took a few steps sideways, eyed me. He wanted to stay, I could tell, but maybe I'm imagining that now. Maybe it's because of what I know.

He took flight, the cool air of his wings on my skin.

But something brought him there.

Like the blowflies.

The ants too.

They marched across the ground, past my feet, like I wasn't even there.

Just like the lambs. Like the fox.

Blowflies and ants and crows.

It was hard to tell what it was at first, beneath the blowflies and ants. I couldn't tell right away.

A voice called to me, from down the hill. Maybe further on.

I stopped, listened.

Nothing more.

Must've imagined it.

Laughter.

I could hear something again, in the clearing.

I had to get away from there.

It just couldn't be.

But I knew.

I knew it was.

And I wanted to run.

I wanted to run as fast as I could. Maybe I should've. I should've run right then.

From Jessie. From the hill. And from him.

I wanted to run more than anything.

Maybe she had the plague. Maybe that's what killed her. Maybe Jessie has it too.

But he wouldn't keep her if she did. He wouldn't want her on the farm. He wouldn't want her with us.

That's what I tell myself.

•

In the clearing.

In the clearing, near the tree, she stood.

'Was she there?'

'Shhh,' I said.

'Is she okay?'

I shook my head. 'She must've gone. She must've left, maybe gone to the town.'

'You sure? Are you sure you looked?'

'Yes.'

It was harder this time. Harder when I don't have as much of the truth.

'Was she sick?' I said.

'Sick?'

'Did she have any lumps?'

'What?'

'Lumps. On her body.'

She frowned.

'What are you talking about?'

So I told her. I told her about the plague and the others. I told her what I knew about the commune and the town. I told her how it's dangerous there.

I told her what he's told me, and how we've been safe here all this time.

I told her how we've been safe, because we're away from the others.

Away from the others and the plague.

We've been trying to get the farm sustainable. We meant to get it sustainable, and she could come live with us. But the drought ruined everything.

And now the others are coming. The others are coming and it's all too late. It's too dangerous.

That's what I told her.

She shook her head.

'He's lying to you.'

That's what she said.

'He's fucking lying to you. None of it is true. There's no plague, there's no nothing.

'We were just hiking. We were on a hike and I fell. My mum went to get help. She went to get help from that fucking psycho!'

That's what she said.

But it doesn't make sense.

I don't believe her.

So I told her to be quiet. I told her to be quiet in case he heard.

'Mum said he was paranoid, but he's just fucking crazy. He's got a gun and a knife and he's . . . he's lying to you, he's telling you lies.'

I didn't believe her.

I *don't* believe her.

'I'll need to put the gag back on,' I said. 'We'll need to put it on and tie your hands, or he'll know.'

Tears ran down her cheeks.

'You're just like him. You're crazy, just like him.'

I was scared.

'He'll be back soon,' I said. 'If he finds out, it'll be worse. It'll be worse for both of us.'

I think she was scared too, because she let me do it.

But first, she made me promise.

She made me promise I'd come back.

But I wasn't sure I would.

I'm still not.

nineteen

He looked at me funny.

He looked at me, and I could see something in his eyes. Something different, again, but I don't know what.

It's nothing I can describe properly. Not with words. More like a feeling, a feeling in my belly.

'You'll have to look it up,' he said. 'Look it up in your books.'

I'd already looked it up, but I wanted to ask. I wanted to see what he'd say.

paranoia
mental disorder with delusions of persecution and self-importance.
abnormal suspicion and mistrust.

I can't imagine why he'd make it all up. I've thought about it, and I can't think that what she said could be true.

She's one of the others, like he said.

Or maybe the people in the asylums. She's probably like that.

One of those two. Maybe both.

No reason why he'd make it all up.

None I can think of.

twenty

This morning, he was gone.

I knew he was gone, because his bedroom door was open. His bedroom was open, and it gave me time.

Time to get the fire going.

Time to make breakfast.

Time for something else.

It's not something I'm proud of, but something I had to do.

Just in case.

I can't write down what it is.

Not yet.

Just in case he finds out.

•

He came back with the sun. I heard him coming up the steps, slowly.

He stood in the doorway. Didn't have his hessian sack.

But he had his rifle.

His knife.

He stood there, silent.

He looked at me for a long time.

'You went there,' he said.

'Where?'

'To her.'

I shook my head.

'I know you did.'

He came inside, closed the door behind him. He placed the rifle on the table.

'Her hands were loose.'

I mustn't have tied her wrists tight enough. But it was hard with the sores. I didn't want to hurt her.

I couldn't tell him this. I couldn't tell him anything.

'Anyway, it doesn't matter now.'

He smiled. Gold tooth.

'We're leaving.'

I didn't say a word, but he saw my thoughts.

'We have to get moving before they come. Can't risk it here any longer.'

The wind blew hard outside, the roof creaked, and I felt the cool air rush in under the door.

The wind was trying to tell the house something, trying to tell me too.

What he was thinking.

What he'd done to her.

So I had to ask.

I had to ask, so I'd know what to do.

'Will she come with us?'

The words stayed in the air. They stayed in the air between us for a long time. And it was forever until he answered.

He shook his head.

'Can't risk it.'

He placed his hand on the rifle, and his gaze drifted somewhere into the distance. Maybe he was looking at my mother, could see her there. Looking at her for one last time.

He took a deep breath, let out a sigh.

'I'll have to deal with it,' he said. 'I'll deal with her on the way.'

twenty-one

If my mother was still here, things would have been different.
    If she was here, he wouldn't be how he is.
He wouldn't be doing the things he does.
If she was here, I wouldn't have to.
I wouldn't have to do it.
That's what I tell myself.

twenty-two

Rabbit traps, oats, matches.

The things he told me to pack.

Things I wanted to take with me too – the *Women's Weekly*, the dictionary, this diary.

Only the things I need. In the hessian sack, like he told me. I slid the sack under my bed.

And I waited until I was sure he was asleep. Until I could hear him snoring in his room, the sound through the house.

Then, I waited longer.

Just to be sure.

•

His snoring and the creaking roof in the wind.

I could hear both these things.

The big knife. The big knife was with me.

I went carefully through the house, as quiet as I could.

Me and the knife.

Across the paddock I went. Past the small dam, past the sheep. Through the fence and up the trail. Up the trail in the dark, with the stars telling me. There was no moon, but the stars were telling me the way like the sailors.

Like Sirena.

Like him.

I went up the trail.

.

I heard her first. I heard, before I saw.

I wasn't sure what it was, but then I knew. I knew once I got close.

She was crying.

Jessie.

She shifted up onto her feet.

I went to her. It was hard to see, but I went in close. I showed her the knife.

'For the gag,' I said.

I carefully reached behind her head, cut the cloth.

'You came back.'

'I promised.'

'Have you seen her?'

'Who?'

'My mum.'

'No.'

'Will he come?'

'I don't know.'

I started to untie her wrists – he'd done it tighter this time. Too tight to get the knife in. My heart pumped hard in my chest. He must've known I'd be back.

My fingers were slippery. Her blood. I tried to be as gentle as I could.

'Shhh,' I said.

The wind was blowing up the hill, away from the house, but I still needed to be careful.

I wondered how long til the sun rose, and if it ever rose early.

I looked to the sky and it was all still stars from the night, and from a thousand years ago.

I got her wrists loose, reached into my pocket.

I crouched down and I found the padlock. I knew about the padlock and the key from his lesson.

But it didn't fit.

I tried it around the other way.

A shrike-thrush called from the bush back down the hill. It was much too early. The sun couldn't come. Not yet.

The padlock clicked.

I unlooped the chain from her ankle.

She was crying again, and I wasn't sure why.

But it felt good.

Even though she was crying, and I knew I was in more trouble than ever before in my life, something felt better. Something inside. A feeling in my belly, my chest.

'Thank you,' she said. 'Thank you so much.'

Her breaths in and out, warm on my skin.

'Where will you go?'

'I'll find someone, someone who can help find my mum. Someone who can take me home.'

'Where's home?'

'A long way from here, but someone will—'

She cried out.

'What is it?' I said.

'My ankle.'

She put her arm over my shoulder.

The shrike-thrush called out again from down the hill, and I wondered if it wasn't a mistake. It knew something I didn't – the sun was close.

He was going through the house, the kitchen.

The rifle with him.

'You have to help me,' she said.

'I can't. I have to go back.'

She shook her head. 'I can't walk on my own. And he'll come. You know he'll come, and he'll find me.'

'I can't. He'll know.'

'He'll know anyway. He'll fucking know when he sees I'm gone!'

'Shhh,' I said.

'You can't just leave me here!'

•

I moved slowly.

I couldn't hear him snoring, and I stepped carefully through the kitchen. It was still dark, so he'd be sleeping. Had to be. He couldn't be up yet.

That's what I told myself.

I found the door. I found it through the darkness, because I was better at it this time.

I knew it almost like him – the house, the farm – in darkness and in light.

I went to my room, stepped over the creaks in the floor. I found the edge of the bed, then reached underneath for the sack.

It wasn't there.

I sat on the bed and slid across to the other side of the mattress. I leaned over the edge and reached underneath.

Nothing.

A sound in the house, a creak.

Just the wind.

It was too late now. Too late to turn back.

I reached further, toward the end of the bed – rough hessian under my fingertips.

I didn't realise I'd pushed it under so far.

Was sure I didn't.

I pulled it out and felt its weight.

The magazine. The diary. Other things.

My chest thumped so loudly, I was sure he would hear. He'd hear my heart and he'd come through the door. He'd see me with the sack, and he'd know. He'd know what I was doing. What I'd done.

I moved slowly back through the house, same way I came.

I listened for his snoring, his breathing, but there was nothing. The house was quiet, like it was holding its breath. It was holding its breath and waiting.

I want things to be better. To be better on the farm, for him and for me. I want him to be better too.

I don't want anything bad to happen to him.

And she promised.

I went down the hallway, through the kitchen, and out into the night.

twenty-three

Three days and three nights now. We've been going as fast as we can.

The last bit I wrote on the second night. I wrote it by the moonlight, when I couldn't sleep. Sometimes the clouds covered the moon, which is why my writing isn't as good. I couldn't keep it on the lines.

I wrote it while she was sleeping. She's sleeping now too.

This is our first fire. I didn't light a fire the first night, because we were too scared. Same the second night. We were too scared he was coming, and he'd smell the smoke.

I was worried he might hear us too, but I know that sound travels slowly. I know from the lessons and the rifle.

I'm still worried about the fire, but we don't have much choice. We don't have much choice because we were too cold on the first two nights. It rained and we got wet, and I've been shivering like crazy.

'We'll get sick,' she said. 'Hypothermia. We have to light one.'

hypothermia
abnormally low body-temperature.

I'm glad I brought the dictionary, even if it makes my sack heavy. She'd told me what it meant, but I looked it up to be sure.

She told me a bit about her family, before she went to sleep. She told me about her mother and her father, how they lived in the commune too.

I already knew from Christine's note, but I didn't say so.

I asked her about my mother, about Elizabeth Taylor.

'I don't remember her.'

I showed her the picture from the *Women's Weekly*, but she still didn't.

'Where is she now?' she said.

'She died.'

'How?'

'I don't really know. Not exactly.'

I didn't want to talk about it much, so I asked about my father instead.

She took a long time to answer.

'I don't remember much, I was too young, but my mum told me things. She said he was . . . complicated.'

That's what she told me.

I still haven't told her though. I haven't told her about what I saw, because it's too late now. I don't want her to be upset.

And I can't be sure, anyway. Not completely.

•

It's been slow going through the bush, and we don't talk unless we need to. In case he's following us, in case he hears.

We try not to go uphill too much, because her ankle is too sore and swollen. She walks with half her weight on me, which makes me tired. She gets tired too.

We don't talk until we set up camp for the night. Until we stop walking.

She asked me some questions. Questions about him, about the farm, and about my mother. About why we came here.

I told her all the answers I knew, but she didn't say very much. She stayed quiet nearly the whole time, and just listened.

Because it was dark, I couldn't see her face. But I wondered what she was thinking, what she thought about the things I'd said.

Before she went to sleep, she promised me again.

I made her promise.

She promised people would come back, and they'd be able to help him.

'He's sick,' she said. 'They'll try to make him better.'

I told her how he got sick once when he cut his fingers, and how his arm swelled up, but she didn't say any more about it.

I didn't tell her about the soft eyes, not right then, because they're too hard to explain. And it's too hard to explain other things too. I'm not sure I want to.

And we both said we'd stop talking.

It was better that way.

twenty-four

W e've gone as far as we can each day. Far as we can with her ankle, and with the hessian sack. At night, we try to find a place away from the trail, somewhere behind the trees and out of sight.

I've been scared. Scared about him coming. The more we've walked, the worse I feel.

I think she's scared too.

We found some water, though. We found it in a creek today, and we drank from it and washed our faces. I wondered if it was the same creek as the one on the hill, but I didn't say so.

It was the nicest water I've ever had. She agreed. And she said water is the main thing.

'You can survive a long time without food.'

And that's when we heard it.

We heard it, and we both knew what it was straight away, without saying.

She put her arm around me, and we left the creek. We went as fast as we could, even though it was hurting her. We went off the trail, then hid under some bushes.

We stayed there, and we listened. We listened for a long time, but there was nothing more.

Even so, I waited til dark before I said it.

Until I thought we were safe.

'He might have just been hunting,' I said. 'For goats.'

She didn't answer.

twenty-five

She looked in my hessian sack tonight, just before she went to sleep. She looked at the *Women's Weekly*, so I told her some more about my mother.

I showed her the picture again, and told her the story about the mink coat, and then about the damper. She listened, but didn't say anything.

She saw this diary too, but I told her it was private.

She saw the rabbit traps, and she made me show her how they work. I showed her what he'd showed me, and even did the test with the stick, so she'd see what they could do.

I told her you have to be careful, because that's what my father told me.

I said we might be able to catch a rabbit, but she doesn't think that'll work.

'Still, they might be useful,' she said.

I wasn't sure what she meant by that.

She hasn't asked about her mother again, and I think she might know. I think she might know, because I heard her tonight. I heard her crying, just before she fell asleep.

But she doesn't know everything. It's probably just as well.

twenty-six

I'd draw a picture, but the fire is getting low, and it's hard to see.

I'd draw a picture, because it's beautiful.

It's beautiful, even though it's so cold and I'm so hungry. The moon and the stars are out, and there's trees around, and there's grass, and it's all so green.

We're lost, and I don't think we'll ever find the road.

I'm sorry I didn't say goodbye.

To my mother. And to him, even if I couldn't.

But if we find the road, I'll come back soon. She promised we'd come back with people from the town, the ones who'll help him. So I'll come too, and I'll see them both then.

But we need to find the road first.

That's what she says.

We need to find the road soon.

Finding the road is hard, because of her ankle, and because we're so tired. But she thinks it can't be far now. Someone on the road will see us, and they'll take us to the town. They'll take us to the town, and then we'll go to Axeville. Axeville is the place where she's from.

That's what she tells me.

But we'll definitely come back. He didn't mean to do the things he's done. Maybe he's sick, like she said, but it's a different kind of sickness. Not like his arm swelling up. It's something else, something inside.

Maybe it's the thing he looks at, the thing he sees inside himself. What he sees with the soft eyes.

I always did the things he told me to. I did them so he wouldn't get the soft eyes. So he wouldn't see that thing inside. But he still did sometimes. He still saw it, no matter what I did.

She looked at me when I told her that. She looked at me and didn't say a word. It was hard to explain. Much harder than his fingers and his arm swelling up.

After a while, though, she said something.

'Did he ever hurt you?'

I looked up to the stars, the stars who'd seen it all. They saw it all a thousand years ago. They know everything.

'No,' I said.

She looked at me.

She looked at me for a long time before she said anything else.

The Others

'They'll make him better,' she said. 'I promise.'
So I've written it down again, so I won't forget.
So she won't forget either.
So they'll have to do what she promised.

part four

one

This is a new diary, but I still have the old one. Ms Lim said I should write in this as often as I can, that it might help.

I see Ms Lim once a week. When I see her, she likes me to call her Jodi, because that's her first name. I've been to see her five times now. She's nice, and gives me a warm chocolate milk and biscuits, and says she'll try to help things get better. She even has a dog with her when we talk, but he mostly sits with me and sleeps. His name is Pickles.

Ms Lim likes it when I talk. She says talking will help, just like the writing.

'Helps process things.'

That's what she tells me.

She asks a lot of questions, and I tell her as much as I can. A lot of people have been asking questions, ever since we came here. Ever since me and Jessie got to the road, which took forever. It took much longer than she thought it would, mostly because of her ankle, but also because we were so lost.

But we didn't have to wait very long once we got there. She was right about that.

A lot has happened since I last wrote anything. More than I could ever have imagined.

I won't write everything, not right now, because there's plenty of time.

It was a truck which came when we got to the road. I'd never seen anything like it. I didn't even know it was called a truck back then, but Jessie told me. It was enormous and loud and had huge tree trunks stacked on the back of it. I've seen plenty of them since.

The man inside the truck was named Gary. He stopped the truck, opened his door, and helped us get inside. He gave us both a drink of water, which was delicious. Jessie drank most of it.

He drove us to Black Gully. Black Gully is a town, but I don't think it's the town my father was going to, because it was too far away.

Gary had a beard like my father, but longer, and a big belly, and he kept saying, 'Fucking unbelievable,' over and over again, and shaking his head. He must've said it about twenty times.

He kept saying, 'Sorry,' after he said it, but I'm not sure why.

The truck went so fast along the road, and Jessie started crying, even though I think she tried hard to keep it in. I was scared, so I asked Gary to make the truck go slower, because

I thought she must've been scared too. So he drove slower and looked over at me sometimes. Sometimes he smiled, and I wasn't sure why, but now I think it was because he wanted me to feel better. He wanted us both to feel better, and not be so scared, but she still kept crying.

After a while, he stopped at a place on the side of the road. It was called *Frankie's*. It had a big sign out front, and there were other trucks just like his, some with tree trunks on the back too. We waited in the truck, and he went inside. He came back out after a little while and gave us each a bottle of orange juice and a ham sandwich. Jessie stopped crying then. Both the sandwich and the juice were delicious, and I've had more of them since.

Jessie asked him if he knew what happened to her mum, but he said he didn't. He said people had been looking for them, but had stopped searching a while back.

'Fucking unbelievable,' he said.

He said this a lot of times.

•

It was a long way to Black Gully, a long way to the town. The town looked a lot different than the picture I did in my diary, how I'd imagined it. I've checked some of my other pictures too, and not all of them were right. Like the cockatoo. Some others as well. I haven't seen a widow's walk yet.

I don't think my father was going to Black Gully to get the oats and bullets, it must've been somewhere closer. When

I asked Jessie, she said he was probably stealing it from farms, but I don't know if this is true.

I was scared when we got to Black Gully. I was scared because of the others and the plague. And I was scared my father would come, but I didn't tell anyone that.

Jessie told me to relax. She told me it was all going to be okay. I tried hard to believe her.

I'd never seen so many people as I saw in Black Gully, but I've seen a lot more since.

The people asked me questions, but they asked Jessie more than me, mainly because she's older. They asked her a lot of things, and some people dressed in dark blue tried to fix her ankle. I didn't know it then, but I know now that they were ambulance people. They fixed it a bit, but not completely. They said it'd get fixed properly back in Hobart.

I'd never seen so many people, and a lot of them wanted to know about what happened to Jessie. But then they wanted to know about me too.

Mainly, they wanted to know who I was.

Who my father was too.

•

When we got taken to Hobart, I'd never seen a place like it. It's hard for me to explain, but maybe I'll do it next time.

I'll have to draw some pictures to explain it properly. It's incredible.

In Hobart, I got asked even more questions by people wearing blue, but not the same ones who fixed Jessie's ankle. These ones were the police. My father said they didn't exist anymore. That wasn't true.

I know now that he said a lot of things that weren't true, but I'm not sure if it was on purpose. Ms Lim reckons it might be because he's unwell, but she said she can't be sure of that, not without seeing him.

I told the police as much as I could, and they wrote a lot of things down. I told them what my father told me. I told them about my mother. I told them about the plague too, but they didn't say it wasn't real. I didn't find that out properly until later, that Jessie was telling me the truth. My father had got it all wrong, but I don't think it was on purpose.

I told them as much as I could about him. I told them they had to go help him, because he needed it.

Because he might be unwell, like Ms Lim says.

And because Jessie promised.

•

The people I've been living with are really nice. They live in Hobart too.

Their names are Bob and Ruth, and they're old and have two sons, but one lives in a place called The Mainland. I haven't been to The Mainland yet, but they've told me they'll take me one day.

They've told me my father is their other son, so they're my grandparents, and I'm their grandson. Their names are Bob and Ruth, but I'm supposed to call them Nan and Pop.

When I called them that for the first time, they started crying. Nan first, then Pop. I'm not sure why.

The house they live in is really nice, and it's warm, and we eat three times a day, and have different things for dinner nearly every time. I even have tuna as a snack sometimes, but it isn't the Sirena one.

It's all strange and different, but good too.

They have a dog named Vic, but he's old like them and doesn't do very much. Even so, I like him. I like sitting with him in the backyard when the sun's out. There's a currawong there too sometimes, in the tree. Just the three of us. They don't have a cockatoo.

They told me I'll be going to school next year, but just for two days a week. Nan told me I'll like it, and that I'll meet other boys and girls there. Boys and girls my age, or even younger. They said if I like it, I'll go more often. They said my reading and writing is really good, so I should have no problems. Ms Lim said so too.

All the lessons must've helped. And the practice my father told me to do in the diary. I told Ms Lim that he'd done lessons with me since I was young, but I didn't say that to Nan and Pop.

They explained how it all works, and I think it's just like the lessons he used to give me, except it'll go for longer.

Even so, I'm looking forward to it.

•

They don't talk about my father much, but they've told me a bit. Mostly it's only when I ask.

Pop goes a bit stiff when I ask, so it's Nan who does most of the talking.

She says my father went his own way in life.

'He was studying at university and doing well, but then it became too much for him. He started to get strange ideas. Put himself under too much pressure, that's what I think.'

That's what she said. Pop didn't say anything.

Nan said they never thought things would end up like they did.

'No one did.'

I know more about the commune now, and about how my father met my mother. Nan and Pop never knew her, but Nan thinks she would have been nice. She said my father and mother both decided to go it alone, that the commune wasn't right for them. But she only knows these things because the police told her.

Once she finished talking about my father, Pop took a deep breath, in and out. He did it just like my father does.

Then, after a while, he said, 'No man is an island.'

I'm not sure what he meant by that.

It was the only thing he said.

Nan says she really wished she'd met my mother. And she said she was sorry things happened like they did. Her eyes got

all shiny when she said it, like she was about to cry, and Pop
got up off the couch and gave her a hug.

They don't do that very much, but it's nice when they do.
Sometimes, Nan tries to give me a hug.

It's okay, but I'd rather watch them do it.

•

Jessie sends me letters sometimes, but hasn't for a while. She
sends letters and I really like reading them.

I never told her about Christine, and she never mentions it.
I think she must know what happened by now, though.

People will have told her.

They probably told her after they found the farm, which took
a while. I told them about my mother too. I showed them the
picture of Elizabeth Taylor, and they found out her real name.

They told me her real name was Carla.

Carla McKenzie.

She has two names, like an actress. Most people do.

I don't know much else about her.

It took the police a while to find the farm, because it's so
remote. That's the word they used.

remote

far away, far apart, distant.

It's another word with more than one meaning, but that's
the right one.

I told them where it was, but it was hard to explain exactly. It's next to a hill, and there's a creek, and it's a long way from the road, and from Black Gully, and from Hobart.

I told them about the sheep and the dams, the rifle, and the fox. I told them about the house too.

I told them my father needed help. He needed help so he wouldn't be sick anymore. The sickness inside of him. What he sees with the soft eyes.

I was worried he might be hurt. He might be hurt because of what Jessie made me do, which I didn't tell them about. I didn't tell the police or Ms Lim.

What she made me do with the traps on the trail.

Like he'd shown me, covered with grass.

She said we had to.

But I don't know if he came looking for us anyway. And I don't know if the traps got him or not, because they haven't said anything. Neither has Nan or Pop.

•

I don't know what happened to my father, and I don't think the police do either.

But they found the farm in the end. They had to use a helicopter, which is the most incredible thing. I think the helicopter was the noise we heard that time, the really loud thunder.

I saw it on the television, which is also pretty incredible. The television doesn't control your thoughts, like he said, but I'll explain it another time when I write.

They found the farm, but my father wasn't there. They looked for a while in the bush, but still couldn't find him. Nan and Pop told me all this after it happened. They told me he'd gone missing.

It all made sense, because he told me we had to leave, but I didn't tell them or the police about that. And I didn't tell them about the gunshot we heard either, but Jessie might've.

I wonder where he might be now, though. I wonder if he's somewhere in the bush. Or maybe he's still looking for me. Maybe he'll get to the road and get picked up by Gary's truck, or by someone else, and get taken to Black Gully. Then he might come to Hobart.

But I think he'd still be too worried about the plague, and the others, even if I know now those things aren't real.

He said it was good to have an imagination, but that's not always true.

I think he's somewhere else now. He's got the rifle and the hollow-points, so he'd be able to hunt for goat and rabbits.

Maybe he's started a new farm somewhere, somewhere no one will find him.

•

It's all so different here, and it's too much to explain right now. It's like another world.

But if I'm honest, even if it was hard on the farm, I miss it sometimes. I miss the sheep, the fox, even the crows. I haven't told Nan and Pop about that. I haven't told them everything.

I miss my father too sometimes, even if he might have done some terrible things. I miss him, and I miss the gold tooth.

Nan said once that he might be gone, that he might be gone to the place of dreams, but she didn't call it that. She said he might have 'passed on', and it took me a while to figure out what she meant.

But I don't think that's true. I feel like I'd know in my belly, my chest, but I can't explain it with words.

I know he's still out there.

I can feel it.

later

I've never driven this road before. By the look, not many have. Carved out of the mountainside. Fire access, most likely.

Haven't driven it before, but I've been here.

The road gets narrower, trees closing in.

My car's not made for this kind of thing, but it's doing the job.

I've got a sense, though. A feeling.

In my belly, my chest.

I'm not far away.

•

I pull over, cut the engine. I sit for a bit, listen to the motor cool and tick. Wind down the window, the crisp air on my skin.

The light's falling, but there's still time.

I grab my swag and the rifle from the boot. Just in case. My backpack too. Phone's inside, but no coverage.

That's okay though.

I know what I'm doing out here, more or less.

Where I'm going.

What I'm looking for.

•

It's more lush than I remember, deep green all around.

The sound of the birds in the trees, lizards scuttling through the undergrowth.

The whole place feels alive, untouched. More alive than before.

I can see the fence line, just up ahead. The posts have mostly fallen down, rotten. The wires dangling loose. No need to pull them apart.

The grass is long in the paddock. And it's green now too – not how I remember.

But some things look the same.

Smaller, but the same.

The dam in the far corner, the reservoir beyond.

Both look pretty full.

Instinctively, I look for the sheep. If I squint my eyes, I can almost see them there, like soft balls of cotton wool in the corner.

Nan and Pop said they got taken by another farmer, one further north. I never knew if that was true.

The house is different, though.

Was never in great shape, but falling to bits now, rotting into the earth.

Boards falling off. Windows broken. Front door kicked in.

The steps have fallen down long ago, but I can still get up there.

Inside, what's left of daylight shines in. Ceiling's gone, rafters exposed. A bird flaps its wings, startled, somewhere in the roof.

Good spot for a nest.

Good place to hide.

Kitchen's been ripped out, just the grimy outline of the cabinets on the floorboards. What's left of them.

In the lounge, even the mantel has been stripped out.

Souvenir hunters, maybe. Teenagers on a dare.

I go to the hallway, your room. I step carefully, avoid the old creaks in the floor. Harder nowadays.

The door's gone, and I peer inside.

Empty.

Floor covered in bird shit.

Even the old cupboard has been ripped out.

The medical book.

The chain.

The padlock.

Down to my room. The door's closed, and I push it, but it's jammed. There's noise inside, movement. I push harder, then give it my shoulder.

It comes free.

A honeyeater flaps madly around the room. Into the walls, once or twice, then out the window. The smell of rotten timber, more bird shit.

It's much smaller than I remember.

Bed's gone, everything's gone.

Not a bad thing.

The loose floorboard, the hiding spot. Still there.

On the wall, graffiti.

Bright red.

FREAKS!!!

Over the window, the fragments of the old sheet. Faded cotton. The dogs and their mirrors.

I look outside. The pit has been filled in long ago, weeds sprouting there. Most of the junk is gone too, maybe for scrap and more souvenirs.

I can see the remnants of the old birdcage. The aviary. My heart gives a thump when I remember. Hadn't thought of her in years.

I look beyond the cage.

Past what's left of the scrap, over the far fence.

Looming above the farm, like it always did.

•

I tried to keep it hidden when me and Jessie got found, but the police checked my sack. They saw it there with the dictionary and *Women's Weekly*, but thought nothing of it.

Maybe they should've.

By the time they might have wanted to see it, I was living with Nan and Pop. And Pop always made sure no one hassled me.

He was good like that.

In the years since, I've never opened it once. I didn't need to remember. Didn't want to.

Until the other morning.

Until I saw the branch in my backyard, leaning against the tree.

And then I found the note you wrote to me, way back then. The note in the back of my old diary. On the very last page. I'd never seen it before.

And I know now what happened. I know that when I went back to get the sack that night, you already knew.

You knew I might leave.

I don't know why you didn't try to stop me. Maybe I was lucky. Maybe you were asleep.

Or you were testing me, to see if I'd stay.

But the *why* doesn't matter so much. What matters is I got away. And what matters is the note you left in the back of my diary.

Because the note is what's brought me here.

You're rotten on the inside, just like the others. Like my family, who tried to twist my mind. Like your mother, who was never happy with our life here.

You've betrayed me, Jacob. Just like your mother did.

And, like your mother, you will be punished.

She tried to run too. But I couldn't let her tell the others about me. About you.

So I found her. And if you leave me, I'll find you too.

I'll come for you, no matter where you are.

Or how long it takes.

And if the others protect you, I'll come for them too.

I will find you.

I'll come for you. And the others too.

•

The sun's only just above the hill now, and I remember how the dark comes quickly here.

Night always came faster for us, on this side.

Sooner for us than the others.

That's what you told me.

I pull my jacket in tight, do up the zip.

If I squint my eyes, I can almost see you. I can almost see you now, up ahead.

The rifle at your side, you turn and smile.

Gold tooth.

•

I climb through the fence.

I stop and look into the gloom of the bush ahead.

The trail.

And something else.

The Others

At first, I don't see it. It takes me a while.

But that's how it's meant to be.

You wouldn't know it's there, unless you knew.

Wouldn't know what it means.

It's there to mark the path, so you know the way home.

I look back to the farm, the house beyond. Soon to be in darkness.

For a split second, a flicker of light.

Candlelight.

Then, it's gone.

·

I go slowly up the trail. The branch in my hand. Rifle slung over my shoulder.

Rimfire.

Hollow-points.

Safety off.

I see another – I can see it up ahead.

I quicken my pace, keep my breath steady.

My heart pumps hard in my chest.

Stay relaxed – if you get tense, you haven't got a hope.

That's what you taught me.

You taught me so much.

The sins of the father.

You made me what I am.

Sometimes, you have to do the most terrible things.

What you did to my mother, to Christine, and the others.

And I know that I'll never be free, as long as you're out there. I'll never be able to leave you behind.

You've been with me, inside me, all this time.

No one can choose how they leave this earth.

You were wrong about so much, but you were right about that.

So I'm not going to wait for you to come. I'm coming for you this time.

Because that's what you taught me.

This time, Father, I'm coming for you.

acknowledgements

I am forever grateful for the wisdom, insight, and friendship of Vanessa Radnidge, who always finds the cracks where the light can get in.

My heartfelt thanks to Deonie Fiford, Stacey Clair, and Boyd Spradbury for again making the writing the best it can be. Deepest thanks also to Gaby Naher and Grace Heifetz, who believed in this story in its early days.

To Louise Sherwin-Stark, Fiona Hazard, Dan Pilkington, Bella Lloyd, Jemma Rowe, and the team at Hachette Australia – thank you for your passion, expertise, and belief in my work.

To Georgia and Millie – your love and support means so much. To my mum – we will endure, though we'll miss Dad forever.

Lastly, I am indebted to Ania Walwicz. You were, and remain, an inspiration.

Also by Mark Brandi

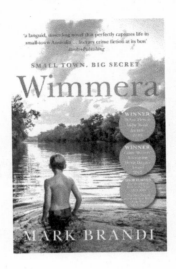

In the long, hot summer of 1989, Ben and Fab are
best friends.

Growing up in a small country town, they spend their days
playing cricket, yabbying in local dams, and not talking
about how Fab's dad hits him, or how the sudden death of
Ben's next-door neighbour unsettled him. Almost teenagers,
they already know some things are better left unsaid.

Then a newcomer arrives in the Wimmera. Up close, the
man's shoulders are wide and the veins in his arms stick out,
blue and green. He looks strong. Maybe even stronger than
Fab's dad. Neither realises the shadow this man will cast over
both their lives.

Twenty years later, Fab is still stuck in town, going nowhere
but hoping for somewhere better. Then a body is found in
the river, and Fab can't ignore the past anymore.

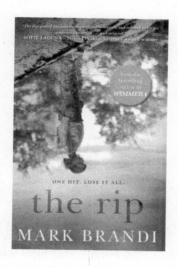

ONE HIT. LOSE IT ALL.

the rip

MARK BRANDI

A young woman living on the street has to keep her wits about her. Or her friends. But when the drugs kick in that can be hard.

Anton has been looking out for her. She was safe with him. But then Steve came along. He had something over Anton. Must have. But he had a flat they could crash in. And gear in his pocket. And she can't stop thinking about it. A good hit makes everything all right.

But the flat smells weird.

There's a lock on Steve's bedroom door.

And the guy is intense.

The problem is, sometimes you just don't know you are in too deep until you are drowning.

hachette
AUSTRALIA

If you would like to find out more about Hachette Australia,
our authors, upcoming events and new releases you can visit
our website or our social media channels:

hachette.com.au

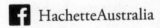 HachetteAustralia

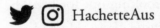 HachetteAus